P9-BIY-760

WITHDRAWN

Love Is the New Black
published in 2014 by
Hardie Grant Egmont
Ground Floor, Building 1, 658 Church Street
Richmond, Victoria 3121, Australia
www.hardiegrantegmont.com.au

All rights reserved. No part of this publication may be reproduced, stored
in a retrieval system or transmitted in any form by any means, electronic,
mechanical, photocopying, recording or otherwise, without the prior written
permission of the publishers and copyright holders.

A CiP record for this title is available from the National Library of Australia.

Text copyright © 2014 Chrissie Keighery
Design copyright © 2014 Hardie Grant Egmont

Design by Belinda Hosford
Typesetting and text design by Ektavo

Printed in Australia by Griffin Press, an Accredited ISO AS/NZS 14001:2004
Environmental Management System printer.

FSC
www.fsc.org
MIX
Paper from
responsible sources
FSC® C009448

The paper this book is printed on is certified against Forest
Stewardship Council ® Standards. Griffin Press holds FSC
chain of custody certification SGS-COC-005088. FSC
promotes environmentally responsible, socially beneficial
and economically viable management of the world's forests.

1 3 5 7 9 10 8 6 4 2

CHRISSIE KEIGHERY

hardie grant EGMONT

1

Piper Bancroft lifted her baseball cap and shook her head to loosen the knots in her long brown ponytail. The flight had been more than three hours, but the two-hour drive to the airport with her mum had seemed way longer in comparison. From the moment they'd pulled out of the driveway, Piper's mum had started on her latest favourite theme. *Grabbing the future with both hands.* For good measure, she included a dash of *onwards and upwards.* Hugely motivational. Piper had especially enjoyed the thinly disguised digs about her relationship with Dylan. She'd been exhausted by the time she even got on the plane.

But now she'd arrived in Melbourne. Piper took a deep breath and stretched up tall as she walked down the airport corridor.

She looked down at her pull-on sand-coloured Converse, watching each step.

This was it. Plan B.

The arrivals hall was crowded with people waiting to greet loved ones and passengers collecting their luggage.

Then Piper saw her godmother, who was actually very hard to miss.

Gaynor held a card in front of her ample chest. A series of glittering gold stars formed a kind of border around the edges of the sign, with Piper's name taking centre stage. With her free hand, Gaynor snapped pictures of Piper, complete with blinding flashes.

Piper smiled and waved, and started walking towards Gaynor. She felt a little embarrassed about all the fuss her godmother was making — people were starting to look at Piper as if she might be a celebrity or something, even though she was just in her favourite pair of faded yellow trackpants and a T-shirt. It was pretty much the usual way she put herself together — she liked feeling comfortable.

Piper felt a little shudder down her spine as she thought of all the new clothes in her suitcase, clothes that were completely different from her normal ones. Not student-type clothes for uni. Not jeans and runners and hoodies. Not Plan-A clothes. Piper hadn't taken clothing advice from her mum since her preference had been fairy dresses and tiaras, but she'd pretty much gone with her mum's thinking on these ones. In her suitcase were outfits she *hoped* would be appropriate for her new job the next day.

'Oh my darling girl, come hither!'

Piper put down her backpack and took in the sight of her godmother. There was a lot to take in. Gaynor was the kind of woman who believed *more is more*. Her make-up was caked on, the kind of make-up she used to wear when she was on stage. It might have looked subtle under stage lights, but it looked over-done up close. Her giant hoop earrings led the way south to a pink-and-gold caftan. From there, the journey down to Gaynor's feet was billowing and flowy and ended at a pair of bejewelled sandals and rings-with-bling on most of her toes.

Piper moved into Gaynor's outstretched arms and let herself be squeezed. Gaynor's welcome card flapped against her face, threatening to knock out any air she managed to inhale.

'I'm so looking forward to having a roommate,' Gaynor enthused, finally freeing Piper from the bear hug. 'It's been . . . '

Gaynor's voice trailed off and Piper bit her lip. She still couldn't believe that Isaac was gone, even though she'd been at his funeral three years ago. It just seemed wrong.

'But are you sure this is what you want, darling?' Gaynor asked, changing the subject.

Gaynor had asked Piper the same question on the phone weeks ago, after Piper's results came in — when she'd realised she might not get into the creative writing and editing course she'd had her heart set on for years. That she was right on the line and it could go either way.

The university had taken her folio and given her an interview.

3

She could still hear the professor's exact words. The words that had plunged her onto the wrong side of that line, into the abyss: *Your marks aren't quite up to scratch, Piper. And your folio, although quite good, doesn't yet demonstrate the level of maturity we're looking for. But you're welcome to try again next year.*

It still felt surreal that she'd stuffed up. Like she'd taken her hand off the wheel for one fleeting second and run off the road. Sure, she hadn't been *entirely* focused around the time of her final exams. And a little bit before that, too, admittedly, while she was preparing her folio. But other than that she'd been a straight-A student forever. She'd figured that learning was like a bank account — that the years of saving it up, *all those years* of being focused, would pay off and get her where she wanted to go.

So much for that theory.

Now it was her two best friends, Sarah and Ally, who were about to start the uni courses they'd dreamed of. They would both be leaving Mission Beach after the summer holidays to go to uni in Brisbane. Ally, Sarah and Piper had planned to share a house.

Piper knew her friends had studied super hard at the end. They'd really hunkered down, rarely going out. But it was different for them; Sarah didn't have a boyfriend and Ally's boyfriend, Harry, was doing his final year too — he wasn't out of school and working and living independently like Dylan.

Now Piper stood watching as luggage circled the carousel.

'This is what I want, Gaynor. Absolutely.' She hoped she sounded full of conviction. She leant her head on Gaynor's shoulder. 'Thanks so much for making it happen, Fairy Godmother. I don't know what I would have done otherwise.'

'You would have done something else,' Gaynor said firmly.

Piper nodded and smiled. It was characteristically generous of Gaynor not to make a big fuss about helping her, but Piper knew that getting a job at *Aspire* would have been the first choice for loads of people. If the job had been advertised, there would have been hundreds of applicants.

Aspire was a fashion and lifestyle magazine. It wasn't that Piper was averse to flicking through a fashion mag, getting the celebrity gossip and stuff. But to actually work in an industry that made women feel shit about themselves, and then sold them products to correct their imaginary faults? Well, it wasn't exactly what she *aspired* to.

Still, she knew she should be counting her blessings. Maybe some time working for a mag like *Aspire* would help on her uni application next year. Magazine work was still in the realm of publishing, even if it wasn't exactly up her alley. Hopefully it would be a stepping stone, another way of getting to where she wanted to go.

Gaynor was giving her was a second chance – since she'd stuffed up the first one so impressively.

Piper saw her suitcase emerge from the chute. She really had to stop thinking like this. Yes, it had been bad timing, meeting Dylan when she did. He'd moved to Mission Beach and into Lofty's house halfway through her final year, and spending time with him became a priority pretty quickly.

But, like Dylan said, *you don't get to choose when you fall in love.*

Luckily, Dylan had been there to comfort her when the exam results came in. He'd been there to point out that not doing so well in your final exams wasn't the end of the world. In fact, he'd been there to love her, to comfort her, whenever she needed him. Even when she'd been stupid and insecure about other stuff.

Piper grabbed her suitcase by the handle and struggled to pull it off the carousel.

'That looks heavy, darling,' said Gaynor. Piper nodded and wished Dylan were here, lifting her suitcase as if it were light as a feather. But she wasn't going to pine for Dylan. He was coming down to stay with her in a few weeks' time. By then, Piper would be on track with her new job. Hopefully, she would ace it. And it wasn't like Dylan had anything against moving to Melbourne. He might have to travel a bit to find good surf, but there was plenty of work for a builder's labourer here. It was just a matter of lining everything up. Things were going to work out fine.

Absolutely.

⌒

Piper sipped on her second glass of champagne while Gaynor drained the rest of the bottle into her own glass. Between them, on the kitchen bench, were instructions on how to get to *Aspire* headquarters.

'And you ask to see Rose McFadden,' Gaynor reminded her.

'What's she like?' Piper asked. Whenever she thought about what the editor of a fashion magazine might be like, she got stressed. She thought of silk scarves, perfectly coiffured hair and military attitudes.

'Oh, she's a force!' Gaynor paused. Piper could see a little smile twitching around Gaynor's mouth as she spoke. 'In the best way.'

This didn't make Piper feel any better. She put down her glass; she really didn't need a hangover on her first day.

'This is an awesome apartment,' she said, getting up from her stool and moving into the lounge room. Gaynor followed her. It was the first time that Piper had ever been there. Gaynor had moved after Isaac died; it was part of her attempt to move on.

The penthouse apartment truly was amazing.

Amazing, as in: huge.

Amazing, as in: 360-degree views of the Botanical Gardens and city skyline.

Amazing, as in: decorated with more animal-fur print than Piper had ever seen outside a zoo.

The blinds were leopard print. There were zebra-skin rugs on the cream carpet. The modular couch was cream, but covered with faux tiger-print throws.

'Yes, it *is* lovely,' Gaynor said, sinking into the couch. She pulled a tiger throw from the armrest and wrapped it around her, as though she was experiencing a sudden chill. Piper couldn't help noticing that Gaynor's eyes had come to rest on a small photo of her and Isaac on the mantelpiece. The photo was taken onstage in a scene from *Who's Afraid of Virginia Woolf?* Piper had seen them in that play. She remembered her parents comparing Gaynor and Isaac to Elizabeth Taylor and Richard Burton, who'd played the same roles in the movie back in the day. Her mum said that Gaynor and Isaac's love was as powerful and passionate as Elizabeth Taylor and Richard Burton's was in real life. Four years ago, at fourteen, Piper had been grossed out at the thought of Gaynor's love life. Too much information.

But now that she had Dylan in her life, she felt like she understood.

Piper's phone buzzed on the coffee table. It was as though Dylan knew she was thinking about him.

Hey babe. You there yet? Miss you already xx

Piper started texting back.

'Dylan?' Gaynor asked.

'How did you know?' Piper looked at Gaynor, surprised.

'The look on your face says it all.' Gaynor patted the couch beside her, and Piper sat down obediently. 'I thought you guys had decided to take a break for a while?'

'I think your information source might be faulty,' Piper replied quickly. 'Neither of us wanted to take a break.'

Piper could hear the defensiveness, the terseness, in her voice. It wasn't Gaynor's fault she thought that. Obviously Piper's mother had put the idea in her head, just like she'd tried to put the idea in Piper's. God, her mum was so judgemental about Dylan.

Even though her mother would never admit it, Piper was sure

her mum was being snobby about him. Just because he hadn't finished school. Because he was a labourer and a surfer and he preferred to live a cruisy life rather than stress about everything. She'd never said it straight out, but Piper could tell her mum blamed Dylan for Piper's results in year twelve. Which was totally ridiculous. If Piper had dropped the ball, if she'd been hanging out with Dylan a bit too much when she could have been studying, that was *her* choice.

'Sorry,' Piper tried again. 'Dylan's going to come down in a few weeks. Then we'll figure out what to do next.'

Dylan was way more than just a labourer. And Piper had the song lyrics — lyrics he'd written just for her — to prove it. Not that she'd ever show anything that intimate to her mother.

Piper would have to fill Gaynor in on what Dylan was *really* like. He was gorgeous and kind and smart in his own way. But she didn't want to start tonight. She didn't want to start out feeling like she was defending him.

'What about you, Gaynes? Is there anyone?' Piper asked, diverting any more Dylan talk.

Gaynor gave Piper a narrow-eyed look. For the moment, at least, she allowed the detour. 'Well, I *have* been doing some internet dating,' she said.

Piper nodded, pretending she hadn't heard all the disaster stories about Gaynor's dating attempts from her mother. Her mum was probably being judgemental about Gaynor's love life, too. 'And how has that been?'

'Good,' Gaynor said quickly, like a reflex. 'Well, it's actually been . . . mixed,' she admitted. She shrugged, a majestic gesture that shed the tiger throw from her shoulders. 'But then,' she said theatrically, 'the course of true love never did run smooth.'

Piper smiled. She'd used that quote in her English essay on *A Midsummer Night's Dream*. But there had been other things she hadn't included. Things that she realised later she should have studied more. Obvious things that had cost her marks.

But all that was over now. That was how Piper had to look at it. There had been a setback; now she was going forward.

Piper's new bedroom was about twice the size of her room back home. It was lovely, though impersonal: wall-to-wall white and beige. The wardrobes were empty except for a couple of blankets and spare pillows. The blanket on the top of the pile was kind of cute: blue with little cartoon ghosts. Piper picked up it up and shook it out. It was a blanket with sleeves.

A Snuggie! thought Piper, giggling and spreading it out on her bed. *Why would Gaynor have one of these? She's so weird!*

She sat down on her bed and checked her phone. There was a message from her mum to see whether she arrived safely.

Then a photo came up on Snapchat. Piper could tell from the background that Sarah and Ally were in Sarah's bedroom, getting ready to go out. Ally was wearing Sarah's stretchy black dress with the cutaway sleeves. Piper smiled, thinking about how that dress had done the rounds. Although the three girls had very different body shapes, the dress fit them all beautifully. Piper had borrowed it for one of her first dates with Dylan. When he'd met her out the front of her house that balmy night he'd looked at her for ages, and then, finally, said just one word: *Smokin'*.

Piper warmed at the memory, and looked back at the photo. Both Ally and Sarah held up cans of Pulse. A cask of wine was on the floor beside them, for when they ran out of the pricey stuff. It was weird to think that her friends were priming themselves for a big night out and she was the one going to bed early. It was a bit of a turnaround from the last months of high school, but, of course, they didn't have to be up early tomorrow morning. They still had a month of holidays to go.

Her friends had included a message with the picture.

Gonna get loose. Wish u were here xx

She stared at the photo, milking the full ten seconds before it disappeared before her eyes. Ally and Sarah weren't exactly party animals. Their version of getting out of it was pretty mild compared to what went on at Dylan's place. But Ally was hilarious after a couple of glasses of cheap wine.

Piper bit her lip. Their last girls' night together had been fun, but it was the type of fun when everything seemed loaded with significance. Where happy could change to sad in a blink. Sarah and Ally would be sharing a house soon – the house that should have been for the three of them. They would be going off to uni each day, and exploring a new life together. Without her. Piper tried to squash down the wave of feelings that arose when she thought about it.

Piper put on the ghost Snuggie and took a selfie to send back. She imagined them getting it and giggling at her Snuggied arm, held up high as though she was dancing, and the caption underneath:

Partying here too. Don't be jealous xx

She quickly unpacked her suitcase and found the card Dylan had given her. She took it with her to the king-sized bed and flopped onto the crisp white sheets.

The card had Dylan's song lyrics written on it. Of course, she knew them off by heart. But still, it was lovely reading Dylan's handwriting and knowing he'd written it just for her.

Piper's Song

Before I met you baby,
life was coloured grey.
There wasn't any loving in my
ordinary day.
Your brown eyes make my heart pump,
it's you that I adore.
If you tell me that you love me,
I'll say I love you more.
Now life is bright and breezy,
you're my one best score.
When you tell me that you love me,
girl, just know I love you more.

Piper slipped the card under the plump pillows and lay back, thinking about Dylan. The day he'd given her the song was the first time they'd gone all the way. She'd been considering it for a while. She'd known Dylan wanted it, but she'd wanted to be sure for her first time. The song had been the clincher.

Piper loved that her first time had been with someone so sensitive; someone she really loved.

Dylan had promised to put the song to music. Piper knew he'd get around to it one day – it didn't matter when.

She had a little piece of him under her pillow.

She grabbed her phone and sent Dylan a bedtime text.

Night. Love u x

His reply came in seconds.

Night babe. Love u more x

Piper had hung her first-day-at-the-office outfit up the previous night and was pleased to see that the creases had fallen out. She put it on and checked herself out in the mirrored doors of the built-in robes.

Her skirt was knee-length and navy. Her collared shirt was white. A thin red belt gave the outfit a splash of colour. It was an outfit that said *serious and business-like*. She hoped. She wasn't in the habit of wearing much make-up, but today she'd applied a touch of foundation and a bit of mascara.

Piper sat on the bed and put on her shoes. Navy sandals with a red strap to match the belt. The heels were about ten centimetres. *Stylish yet serviceable*, she told herself.

But it was the handbag that Piper was most pleased with. She'd actually seen the bag in the fashion pages of last month's *Aspire*. It was a Marc Jacob classic: a huge Hillier Hobo. *Pretty ironic to call it a hobo bag when it's worth more than what most people I know earn in a week,* thought Piper.

She'd bought it online at half the advertised price, but still, it was the most expensive thing she'd ever bought for herself. It was worth it, though. Having the gorgeous bag hanging off her arm made her feel like she might pass as professional.

Gaynor had left breakfast stuff out on the kitchen bench, but there was no way Piper could eat. She managed to figure out how to use the Nespresso machine, found a takeaway cup to put it in, grabbed the print-out of the directions to work and headed out the door.

Getting to Southbank was easy: just a tram and a little bit of a walk. Piper checked the time on her phone. It was only 8 a.m., yet the banks of the Yarra River were buzzing. Buskers were setting up. People walked with intent, swerving around those who looked like they had a lazy day to play with. To her right, a boat chugged past on the river, a white wake stretching behind it. It was all happening. In Mission Beach at 8 a.m., it would be dead quiet.

The city buildings all seemed so grand, somehow. It was beautiful. Piper drank it all in as she walked, hardly believing she was really there. She stared across the river at the old facade of Flinders Street Station, at the tall buildings, imagining all the important people inside doing important things.

The city was so full of possibility that Piper couldn't help feeling swept up in it. She looked to her left and took a deep yoga breath to centre herself.

This was it. The headquarters of *Aspire*.

The revolving glass door seemed to speed up as soon as Piper entered. The spinning glass wall hit the heel of her sandal and propelled her forward. She didn't so much exit the revolving doors as get spat out.

She was thrust into someone in front of her and instinctively grabbed onto them to stop from falling over.

'Not used to the pace?' came a voice.

Piper barely looked up. Extracting her hands from the torso of a complete stranger, a complete *male* stranger, was keeping her busy enough.

'Oops,' she said, just about to apologise when she realised the guy was already walking off. She could only see the back of him. Dark, wavy hair. Broad shoulders. Grey T-shirt. Mustard chinos.

Very nice from behind, she thought, recovering herself. *But what was with that comment?* Piper was actually glad she hadn't had time to apologise.

Piper strode towards reception, making sure to pull herself up to her full height, following the instructions her yoga teacher at home had taught her. Since Piper was only 150 centimetres tall, this was pretty important. Still, even at her full height, she felt decidedly tiny.

The reception desk was about three metres long. Behind it sat three incredibly gorgeous women. They sat so evenly spaced behind the expanse of desk that it could have been measured with a ruler. One had white-blonde hair, one bright auburn and the third, jet black. It looked as if they'd been given their jobs based on hair colour. *Surely that's a violation of anti-discrimination laws*, thought Piper.

Behind the receptionists was a giant, curved plasma screen. Tall, stick-figure models with big hair and impossible cheekbones pelvic-thrusted their way down a runway. Piper paused for a moment to check out the way their feet crossed in front of each other as they walked. As each model took centre stage, her name and measurements appeared in a caption at the bottom of the screen. Currently the caption read:

Maddison Brown: Height 177 cm, Bust 79 cm, Hips 90 cm, Dress 8, Shoe 10.

It's like they're for sale, Piper thought. *Line up, girls, and show the buyers what you've got.*

She looked back to the receptionists, who were tapping away at sleek computers, barely acknowledging her existence.

Piper cleared her throat. 'Um, I'm starting work today. Piper Bancroft,' she said. The auburn-haired girl looked up, clearly underwhelmed by this information. 'So, I need to meet with. . .'

At the sound of a heavy rumble, Piper turned to look behind

her. A giant crate on wheels was being pulled through reception. Piper couldn't help but wonder what was inside.

'This needs to be signed for by management,' the delivery guy told the receptionists, handing over a delivery slip.

The black-haired receptionist nodded and dialled a number immediately.

'Oooh, this has to be the McQueen gown,' the blonde receptionist cooed.

'Ostrich feathers,' the auburn-haired woman replied knowingly.

The next few minutes were a whirlwind of activity. A stylish-looking girl with white-blonde hair that was shaved on one side and shoulder length on the other came down to collect the crated gown, pausing to give the receptionists a teeny glimpse inside the crate. Piper strained to get a look too, but her view was blocked by a group of male models telling the auburn-haired receptionist they were late for a shoot. Piper was surrounded by biceps and triceps and pecs and abs. The scent of cologne was so overpowering it almost made her dizzy.

Finally, everyone cleared out.

On screen, Maddison Brown had toppled over her size 10 stilettos and was now looking extra colt-like in her attempt to get up. Piper knew how Maddison Brown felt. *Awkward*.

Auburn Girl stared at Piper blankly.

'Um . . . with Rose McFadden,' Piper managed.

Following Auburn Girl's instructions, Piper walked down the corridor, counting the doors on her left as she went. She felt like she was running the gauntlet: she passed between two photographers arguing about the best location for their shoot; and a rack of clothes, seemingly with a life of its own, pushed past her so that she had to stand aside or be run down. She managed to duck inside an open door to let the stampede of male models she'd seen before pass by. She wasn't sure she'd ever be seen again if she got inside *that* scrum.

The plate on the doorway read *Art Department*. Piper was a little surprised. She'd expected an art department to look, well . . . *arty*. But this room was pretty plain. Two girls were at the far end of the room and a guy sat, with his back to her, close enough for her to see his screen. He was mucking around with a page from the magazine, changing fonts and shifting pictures. Piper checked the corridor to make sure it was clear and exited before anyone even looked up.

Finally, Piper stood at the half-open door to Rose's glassed-in office. The plate on the door read *Editor in Chief*. Piper gave a timid knock.

A woman she supposed to be Rose was leaning over her desk, looking at hundreds of images. She started talking without looking up.

'Viv, I've narrowed it down. There are only three possible covers, really. This one is probably my favourite because the model's cheekbones beautifully echo the jagged geometry of the . . .'

Piper stepped into the office, feeling like an interloper. Well, *being* an interloper, actually, since Rose obviously thought she was someone else. She hadn't looked up, even for a moment.

Piper glanced at the photos on her desk. They all looked pretty much the same to her: a very beautiful, sharply angular model with a crew cut rose out of a waterfall, somehow staying completely dry and glam in gold chiffon. Rose pushed most of the photos to the side until there was only one left in front of her.

'Actually, Viv, this is definitely the one. Of course it is!' Rose said it like it was a eureka moment. She lifted the photo in the air and finally looked Piper. 'Oh. You're not Viv,' she said, her face falling.

'Ah, no,' Piper replied. 'Sorry.'

It wasn't a great first impression, apologising for not being someone else. Piper could almost feel the domino effect it might have. God, what would she be doing next? Apologising for being here at all?

'Never be sorry for not being someone else,' said Rose. She walked around her desk and Piper was finally able to see her properly.

It was funny. Piper had expected sharp edges, but instead Rose was sort of soft-focus. Her hair was a mass of wild, blonde curls. Her eyes were hazel and her lips full. She wore a long, flowing printed dress and loads of bangles.

'I'm Piper. You know my godmother, Gaynor Tremorne?' Piper offered. For a second, she wondered if Rose even remembered she was starting today.

'Ah, yes! Of course,' Rose agreed. She floated back behind her desk and motioned for Piper to take a seat in the chair opposite.

'Gaynor,' she said slowly, 'was on the cover of *Aspire,* my first cover as editor.' Rose paused, remembering. 'Everyone said she was too old. Everyone told me to use a model, not an actress. Yet, it was the best-selling *Aspire* that whole year. Gaynor is like a good luck charm to me.'

She looked at Piper strangely, almost as though she was hoping Piper might also be a good luck charm. *For what, though?* Piper wasn't sure. She was probably reading too much into a look. Like Dylan said, sometimes she got carried away with over-analysing things.

'I'm really looking forward to this job,' Piper said, bringing herself back to reality. 'Thanks for giving me a chance. I'm happy to do anything you need –'

As she spoke, Piper heard the click-clicking of high heels entering the office behind her. She paused and turned around. The girl behind her was quick to fill the silence.

'Rose, you have a management meeting in the boardroom at one. I've booked a Skype with Alex Perry at three to discuss a spread for his Frockaholic range for the August issue. Cocktails at seven o'clock with the features crew and Jennifer to thank her for coming in for the interview and shoot –'

'Aniston or Lawrence?' Rose interrupted.

'Aniston. We're still working on Lawrence. I'll send you your program for the day.'

If Piper had been waiting for someone with hard edges, this girl met that expectation and raised it one. She could only have been a few years older than Piper. Her hair was black, except for the ends, which had been dip-dyed bright blue. She was incredibly tall, thin as a rake, and wore a tight black dress with killer high boots. Her lips were bee stung and bright red. A sleeve of tattoos ran down her left arm. The tiger on her bony upper arm held Piper's attention.

'Thank you, Vivian,' Rose said. She motioned a bangled arm towards Piper. So far, Vivian had managed to ignore her completely. 'This is Piper, the girl I told you would be starting today,' Rose said. 'I have a good feeling about her. Piper, this is Vivian Jacobson.'

Piper smiled at Vivian. In return, she received a head-to-toe scan, finished with a subtle eye roll. Piper had a sense that Vivian didn't care much for Rose's *feelings*. Rose didn't seem to notice.

'Oh Rose,' Vivian said, 'not another intern? I've just got rid of Henry or Harry or whatever his name was and now we've got another pasty soul who's flounced in from *fashion college* with zero idea of how the world really works. Honestly, I know they're free, but half the time these work experience students couldn't do up a shoelace, let alone be any real help.'

Piper stood there feeling awkward.

'Piper's not an intern,' Rose said to Vivian, her smooth voice a huge contrast from Vivian's snappy one. 'She is a friend's goddaughter, and now she is our employee. Piper will assist you until we work out where she's best placed.' She turned to Piper and smiled. 'I'd be lost without Viv, you'll learn a lot from her.' Then she looked down at the pictures on her desk. 'Right. I need to finalise this cover with the art department,' she said, floating out of her office and leaving Piper alone with Vivian. The temperature in the room seemed to plummet below zero.

Without a word, Vivian walked out of Rose's office and started down the corridor. She snapped her fingers over her shoulder, in what appeared to be an instruction to follow. Piper practically had to break into a jog to catch up.

'So, what can I do with you? Or at least, what can I give you to do so I don't have to babysit?' Vivian hissed as she walked.

Piper tried not to react. *Babysit.* 'You give me a job and I'll do it,' she said, hoping she sounded strong and confident.

Vivian almost looked amused. At least, the corners of her fire engine—red lips lifted slightly. She paused at the door of a large but windowless office.

Inside, a girl sitting in front of a computer looked up and gave Piper a wave and a smile. Piper recognised her as the girl who had come into reception to collect the ostrich gown.

'Your computer,' Vivian said, pointing to a Mac on a small empty desk beside the girl. Then she waved in the direction of a hatstand in the corner of the office that was groaning under the weight of coats and bags.

'Hang up your coat and your fake Marc Jacobs and I'll go try to find you something you can do,' said Vivian, before disappearing down the hall.

3

'Don't worry,' said the girl at the computer, gesturing towards Piper's bag. 'Thousands of people have made the same mistake.'

Piper tried to turn her grimace into a smile.

'Real Marc Jacobs bags never have a metal tag hanging off them. The logo tag is always on the actual bag. Other than that, it's a pretty good copy.'

Piper fingered the tag that hung from her handbag, wishing she could cut it off. She tucked the bag way underneath her desk and then gave it an extra shove with her foot. Out of sight.

'I'm Lucy,' the girl continued. 'Junior fashion stylist.'

It figured. Lucy looked even more stylish up close. Tribal swirls were carved into the shaved side of her white-blonde hair. She wore soft-looking print leggings and a baggy cream T-shirt. Piper ran her hand down the length of her plain brown hair.

'I'm Piper, and I have no idea what I am,' she said.

Lucy grinned. There was a piercing in the middle of her tongue that made Piper wince a little. Getting her ears done had been hard enough for her.

'Ah, I'll give you a little clue,' Lucy said, getting up from her desk. Piper followed her to the other side of the room. Lucy opened some sliding doors. 'You are now in the fashion cupboard, the hub and centre of any self-respecting fashion mag.'

Piper's jaw dropped as she walked inside. It was more like a room than a cupboard. Piper had never seen anything like it. Hundreds of pairs of shoes lined the floor amongst mountains of cardboard boxes and coathangers. Dozens of hats were on the top shelves, some standing alone and others stacked up on top of each other. In between, there were racks of clothing sticking out at all angles. A giant poster of an *Aspire* cover in heavy cardboard leaned precariously against a rack of clothing. Piper had seen the episode of *Sex and the City* where Carrie got to go inside the fashion cupboard at *Vogue*. This was similar, but much, much more chaotic.

As if to demonstrate Lucy's point about the fashion cupboard being a hub of activity, a short, bronzed guy with a white Mohawk haircut power-walked in. Behind him, a tall, sturdily built girl wearing a kimono-style grey dress, her brown hair piled high on her head, pulled a suitcase on wheels. 'Wardrobe malfunction on the McQueen shoot,' the Mohawk guy said, flicking some invisible lint from his impeccable black suit. 'I need Jimmy Choos. Size eleven. Life or death.'

Piper stood back as Lucy fished out a box and handed it to the guy. It only took her a moment, making Piper suppose that the chaos might be a bit more organised than it seemed.

'I worship at your feet Lucy,' the guy said, already exiting with the box. 'See you there.'

'I *think* the stuff in here could be the accessories for the Dinnigan shoot,' the kimono-clad girl said as soon as Mohawk had gone. She looked flustered as she tapped at the suitcase. 'I didn't really hear Vivian properly and I totally wasn't game to ask again.'

Lucy shook her head. 'That's okay, Bronwyn, I'll check it out,' she said.

Bronwyn looked as though Lucy had given her a reprieve, and she scuttled out.

'Albert is freelance,' Lucy explained. 'He's doing make-up trials for our Alexander McQueen shoot at the Botanical Gardens next week. He's the best in the business. Bronwyn's one of our interns. She's studying to be a fashion designer and she's in her second week of work experience.'

Lucy and Piper stepped out of the fashion cupboard and sat back down at their desks.

'Well, as you may have guessed by now,' Lucy said, 'you've landed in the fashion department. In full, that would be fashion, beauty and health. If you've got Vivian setting your agenda,

I'd say you'll just be doing as you're told, like we all do.'

Piper's heart sank a little. The fashion cupboard was cool, and any girl would kill to comb through its contents. Plus, Lucy seemed really lovely, and it was clear from her interactions with Albert and Bronwyn that she was being modest in saying she only did what she was told. But Piper had really hoped to land in the features department, where she knew the in-house articles for the magazine were created. Even if the articles Piper had come across in *Aspire* were just fluffy, feel-good pieces, they were still *published* fluffy, feel-good pieces. At least she'd be doing *something* to develop her writing skills.

'So, do you write your own pieces in the fashion department too?' Piper asked. Lucy shrugged in sort of half-agreement, nodding in greeting at a chic-looking woman scurrying past to the fashion cupboard. 'Do you think there's a chance I'd get to actually *write* anything for the fashion section?' Piper continued, feeling humbled about lowering her expectations even further.

'Yeah, sure,' Lucy laughed. She bit her lip as though she wasn't happy with herself for the sarcasm that seemed to seep out of her last comment. 'Sorry. That was unprofessional. Vivian does the fashion copy,' she added seriously.

Despite Lucy correcting herself, Piper could tell that she thought there was zero chance Piper would be contributing *any* writing about *anything*. It was a pretty depressing start.

But she *was* glad, at least, that Lucy was taking the time to explain things.

'Don't worry, you can at least be sure that Vivian will keep you busy,' Lucy continued. 'Rose is the visionary. She has the lofty and lovely ideas for the whole mag. Vivian's the head of the fashion department. So she makes things like fashion shoots happen.' Lucy tilted her head to the side. 'Vivian is just a bit stressed at the moment, because there's still heaps to organise for the Dinnigan shoot at sunset today.' She tapped her tongue stud against her teeth. 'Well, actually, Vivian is pretty stressed generally,' she corrected herself. 'Getting all the departments in sync to get the mag out on time is always pretty full on. But it's been an extreme sport since Mason Wakefield took over and started cost cutting.'

Piper nodded, taking it all in. 'Who's Mason Wakefield?'

Lucy bit her fuchsia lip. 'Mason is the new boss. The CEO. Well, kind of. He's the heir apparent of *Aspire*,' she explained. She looked around to ensure no-one was within earshot. 'Our real boss, Patrick Wakefield, is his dad. But Patrick's on an extended holiday or something. If you believe the rumours, he's had some kind of breakdown. But he's probably just on some island drinking martinis while we're left here to bust our guts.

'Anyway, now his son has rocked up with his MBA from Harvard. And he's been slashing budgets and sacking people. He calls it *streamlining*. He even got rid of our champagne fridge, if you can believe that. He keeps talking about working smarter, not harder. But in the meantime, we're all just running around like chickens without heads, trying to meet deadline with half the usual budget.'

Piper screwed up her nose. 'So if he's sacking people, and he's got interns working for free, why did they employ me?'

'Ah, let me guess,' Lucy said, tapping her temple. 'How old are you?'

'Eighteen,' Piper replied.

'Well, you're young. Inexperienced. *Cheap*. And interns don't generally stick around for long, since they normally have other commitments with their studies. Think of yourself as slave labour. Just another example of Mason Wakefield's brilliant *streamlining*.' Lucy rolled her eyes.

'Okay, I think I've got that. Mason equals . . . ' Piper mirrored Lucy's eye-roll.

'Correct,' Lucy laughed.

'And what's the story with the sunset shoot?' Piper asked.

'Well, Miranda pulled out at the last minute because Flynn has a cold,' Lucy said, looking up at the woman who had emerged from the fashion cupboard with a feathered headdress and was gesturing at Lucy with it. 'Yes, that'll be fine, Siobhan,' she smiled, then continued. 'But apparently we've been able to score Kara Kingston at short notice. It's quite a coup since you normally have to book ahead for aeons to get her.'

Piper nodded. She wasn't big on following the careers of models, but you'd have to be on another planet not to know who Kara Kingston was. If Piper was asked to picture a model, Kara would have been the first one to spring to mind. She'd been on zillions of magazine covers, but she was most famous as the longest serving, and arguably the hottest, Victoria's Secret Angel.

29

Piper could understand why. Kara Kingston had a killer body and a beautiful face. But there seemed to be something *extra* cool and collected about her. When she stared out from a magazine cover, she looked completely self-possessed. In fact, on one cover Piper had seen, Kara spun the world on her fingertips. Granted, it was just a globe, but the message was clear. Kara might be from Down Under, but she had the X-factor to make the world sit up and pay attention.

'So this shoot is pretty important?' Piper ventured.

'Totally,' Lucy said. 'If we can get a shot to put on the front cover it will guarantee –'

'Seriously, Lucy,' Vivian's voice cut through the office, 'you have time to chat? How lovely for you.'

It was weird how Vivian just seemed to *appear*. Even weirder was the fact that a little pug dog with a studded collar, dressed in a silver silk jacket, was standing next to her.

'So, I'm assuming you've sourced the twelve bikinis in shades of the sun for our "Summer Sun" piece? And you've got all the pant-lengths extended for Brianna Cole's McCartney shoot, since her legs are about twice the length of the pants?'

'I'm getting onto that now,' Lucy said. 'Right away, Vivian.'

'Not so fast,' Vivian hissed. 'Kara Kingston has somehow managed to get legless. You need to get to the Langham and sober her up for the shoot. Larry's there with her at the moment. See if he needs anything. If he has to have a toilet break, give him five minutes. Stay with her until her agent arrives.'

Piper tried not to let her expression register her surprise. It was kind of early to need sobering up.

Lucy took in a deep breath, as if she was going to say something, but then stopped herself.

'Now, you,' said Vivian, looking at Piper and rolling her eyes. 'Take Rose's dog for his walk.'

As soon as the little dog heard the word *walk*, he started wagging his curly little tail. It wasn't exactly what Piper had planned for her first day, but at least the dog was seriously cute.

'What's his name?' Piper asked.

Vivian sighed loudly, as though the question didn't warrant an answer.

'Excuse me. Vivian?' Lucy ventured. 'Do you think that maybe Piper could go and check Kara? It's just . . . if I go to the Langham I'm not going to be able to finish all the stuff I need to do here.'

Piper's heart skipped a beat. She could have hugged Lucy on the spot. Imagine meeting Kara Kingston!

Vivian, not making way for the stream of people passing her to get to the fashion cupboard, put her hands on her uber-slim hips. As she did so, the poor little pug was dragged towards her on his lead. She shook her head. 'It's too important,' she said sternly. 'If you can't cope then I guess I'll have to do it myself.'

Piper resisted the urge to roll her eyes. It was as though Vivian was annoyed with Lucy for not being able to be in two places at once. She seemed hell-bent on underestimating Lucy and bullying everyone else. Helping sober someone up wasn't rocket science.

Piper cleared her throat. 'I can do it. It wouldn't be the first time I've helped sober someone up.'

'Oh, the eighteen-year-old Woman of the World,' Vivian sneered. She shook her head. 'I guess I don't have much of a choice since Lucy is busy and we're on skeleton staff.'

Thanks for the vote of confidence, Piper thought.

'Okay, go,' Vivian said reluctantly. 'And take this thing with you.' She added, as though the dog were a lump of wood. 'But Piper,' she warned, looking at her sternly, 'Kara Kingston *cannot* be left alone. Do *not* give her the chance to have a drink. Empty the minibar. Check her room. Check her handbag. Check her pockets. Check her freaking *cavities* if you have to. God knows she's good at hiding those mini bottles. Get it?'

'I get it,' Piper responded.

'Believe me. You fuck this up, you do *not* get a second chance.'

Piper took the leash quickly, before Vivian could change her mind, and turned back for a moment to grab her bag. She'd really done a good job of tucking it way, way under the desk. She had to crouch down, the dog pulling her towards the door by her right hand, her left searching underneath the desk.

'Interesting thing to say,' Piper heard a male voice say just as her hand touched the fake label on her fake Marc Jacobs bag. At this point, her butt was sticking out into the office while her head was shoved under the desk.

'*Fuck this up, you do not get a second chance*,' continued the voice. 'Maybe I should get some posters printed, since some people seem to be fucking up a lot and yet still get second chances.'

The dog tugged hard on the leash, yanking Piper out from under the desk. The leash flew out of her hand and the dog jumped up excitedly on the guy's leg. Piper saw the mustard chinos. Her heart pounded in her chest as she registered, from the ground up, mustard chinos, grey T-shirt, broad shoulders, dark wavy hair.

The guy glanced over to Piper as she stood to her full height. *Jesus.* His emerald eyes were piercing, and seemed busy skewering Vivian. Piper was glad he didn't seem to recognise her from earlier. She noticed that Lucy was setting a cracking pace at her keyboard. *Boss-in-the-office* pace.

'I am so sorry, Mason.' Vivian's whole demeanour was different. The condescending tone was gone. Her hands were balled up into fists but her voice was controlled and soft. 'I was under the impression that the Kate Spade bags were to be used for the "In the Bag" shoot and then both the dresses and bags were to go back to New York.'

'Correct,' said Mason. 'Except that two dresses, two *sample* dresses that haven't even been put into production yet, and two very pricey handbags, never made it back to New York. Which is anything *but* correct.'

God, this guy was *intimidating.* It would have been smart to at least look away. To look down, or at her computer. But something about him made that impossible. Piper couldn't help noticing his perfect abs, easily visible under his soft grey T-shirt. His biceps popped out of his sleeves so it looked like he was flexing, without even being aware of it, as he addressed Vivian. He would only be in his early or mid-twenties. His voice was even and controlled, but had an edge to it, as if he was talking to someone who was completely incompetent.

'Look,' Vivian said, 'in some ways Lucy is just learning. There's a lot of pressure on her to get everything sorted after ... '

As soon as she heard her name, Lucy stopped typing. Her fingers remained poised above her keyboard as if she was frozen.

Vivian had trailed off, as though she realised there was no excuse that would cut it with Mason Wakefield. She tried another tack. 'Mason, as head of the fashion department, I know the buck stops with me. It won't happen again,' she finished.

Funny how she managed to blame Lucy and take the high road at the same time, Piper thought.

Just then, the dog started whimpering.

'Would anyone like to tell me why there is a dog loose in the fashion department?' Mason asked.

But Piper was surprised to see him reach down and scratch the dog fondly between the ears. The pug gave a snort of satisfaction that was pretty loud considering the size of the dog.

'Hey, Bruno. It's okay, buddy,' said Mason. Then he grabbed the dog's leash and held it out to Piper. 'You might need this.' As Piper took it, he kept hold of it so she couldn't go anywhere. 'Just watch out for the revolving doors on your way out,' he said, before letting go.

4

Piper stood outside the doors of the Langham Hotel. She should have thought ahead. She'd promised Vivian that she'd look after Kara Kingston — whatever that involved — but she hadn't thought about what she was going to do with Bruno when she went inside the hotel. As far as she knew, five-star hotels didn't welcome pets. The problem was, she hadn't been able to think straight. She kept thinking of Mason's comment.

Watch out for the revolving doors on your way out.

It was bad enough that she'd accidentally groped the guy who turned out to be the boss on her very first day at *Aspire*. But that he drew attention to her little disaster and rubbed it in like that? It was just too much. Even now, hours later, she was mortified.

At least he recognised me, she thought, trying to find the bright side, although she wasn't quite sure why that was important. Especially as he recognised her for all the wrong reasons. God, how had she managed to mess up on her first day?

She had a sudden pang of longing for Dylan. She momentarily wished she could be back at Mission Beach, where everything was familiar and safe.

Snap out of it, Piper, she told herself. *You never wanted to stay there. This is an amazing job. You're about to meet Kara freaking Kingston!*

She looked at the pug and back at the Langham. Then she opened her bag. There had to be *something* positive about getting the extra-large Hillier Hobo bag. Even if it was a fake.

Piper stepped out of the elevator and into the foyer of the penthouse suite. It was decorated with the biggest bouquets of flowers she'd ever seen; they almost touched the ceiling.

She knocked on the door and an enormous bodyguard appeared. He looked ex-army, with a buzz cut and bulging muscles.

'Thank god you're here!' he gasped in a hushed tone as soon as he saw Piper, relief flooding his face. 'I don't get paid enough for this.' He took a deep breath and Piper could tell he was trying to calm down. 'Sorry. I'm Larry.' He held out his hand and Piper shook it.

'Piper,' she said. His grip was fierce.

'I rang her agent,' Larry explained rapidly in a low voice, 'but she can't make it here for another couple of hours. Kara was pretty bad when I first got here. Off her face. She's a bit better now, but I wasn't sure what to do. She's been crying, and all over the place and . . . this ain't in my job description, you know?' Larry paused. He took another breath. 'I made her a cup of tea,' he added, looking at Piper as though she might be able to confirm this was the right thing to do. He looked completely out of his depth.

Piper bit her lip. If Larry was out of his depth, then she was about to dive into the ocean without a buoy in sight.

'Bloody newspaper article set her off, I reckon,' Larry continued, breaking into Piper's thoughts. 'Room service must've brought it up with breakfast before I arrived. I tried to bin it, but she's obsessed. Won't let me touch it.'

Piper's bag rustled. For a second, she considered using the dog as an excuse. *Sorry, Larry, but I'm going to have to come back later. I forgot I had a dog and all.* She could reverse her way back into the elevator, back outside, back to *Aspire* headquarters. But Larry had already turned around and was entering the suite.

'Kara,' he called in a cheerful voice. 'Piper's here to take care of you. Okay, love?' The relief in Larry's voice was palpable.

The Kara Kingston in front of Piper wasn't cool, collected or self-possessed. She was flopped on the couch, her eyes closed. She wore a tatty old pink terry towelling dressing gown. On her feet, though, as if to declare that she was, in some ways, dressed, she wore a pair of boots. Amazing boots, really. Piper had never seen anything vaguely like them. They were emerald-green snakeskin with a yellow trim around the top and a cowboy heel. Even in her dishevelled state, with puffy dark rings under her closed eyes. Kara was stunning.

Although the suite was grand and spacious, with floor-to-ceiling windows along one wall and beautiful parquet floors, the place felt chaotic. The couch was littered with used tissues. Beside Kara on the coffee table was a tacky tabloid. Piper looked at the front page.

Young Mag Mogul Dumps Our Kara?

Piper stifled a gasp. Mason Wakefield was Kara's boyfriend?

The photo had been taken outside a nightclub, judging by the queue of people and the rope rail. Mason Wakefield was in the background. Piper couldn't see his expression because he had a hand up, shielding himself from the camera. She could definitely see Kara's face, though. Kara was crying, her beautiful face crumpled. There was a sense of motion about her too, a slight blur around the arms. A woman with long blonde hair was in the foreground. It looked like Kara was trying to escape from Mason and catch up with the girl.

Piper sucked in a breath. She scanned the article.

How much can Kara Kingston take?

Seen last week leaving the Cristobel Club at 2 a.m., Kara broke away from mag mogul Mason Wakefield. Sources say Kara was comforted by a good friend, DJ Laurie Anderson. Neither Kingston nor Wakefield was available today for comment, but Kingston's agent, Anita Barnes, insists it was just a lovers' tiff.

Do you think Kingston should ditch Wakefield for good? Take the poll at insiders.com.au.

Piper looked up at Kara. Even with her eyes closed, she could see pain etched across her forehead. Mason Wakefield was causing destruction all over the place. She wondered what he'd done to Kara at the nightclub. Who was he to go around breaking supermodels' hearts, *streamlining* businesses and making unsuspecting new girls feel completely inadequate? What an arrogant jerk!

She put the paper facedown on the coffee table and, very gently, shook Kara's arm to wake her up.

Kara awoke with a start. 'Jesus. Who are you? Where's Larry?'

Piper took a step back. 'Hey, Kara,' she said, hoping her tone was soothing. 'Larry is taking a break. I'm from *Aspire*. Vivian sent me to ... help.'

Kara stared at her blankly. 'If you want to help,' she said slowly, 'then can you do me a favour?' She grabbed the tabloid from the coffee table and held it against her chest.

'Sure,' Piper said.

'Leave me alone,' said Kara. She lay back on the couch and closed her eyes again.

Piper tiptoed over to the bar fridge with the Bruno bag still slung over her shoulder and checked the contents. There were only soft drinks and juices. Piper supposed she was a little too late to follow Vivian's instructions to make sure there was no alcohol within Kara's reach.

She tiptoed back to the couch, totally unsure of what to do next.

Suddenly, Bruno snorted loudly.

Kara opened her eyes with a start. 'What the fuck was that?' she asked. She stared at Piper as though waiting for the noise to come again so she could figure out exactly what it was.

Piper pointed to her handbag. Bruno's head was sticking over the top.

When she saw Bruno, Kara's face changed. A weak smile played on her lips, giving Piper a glimpse of the famous gap between her front teeth.

'He does that sometimes,' Piper said. Without thinking, she did an imitation of Bruno snorting.

Kara's smile grew. She held out her hands and Piper passed Bruno to her.

'So, what is this, pet therapy?' Kara asked, scratching a contented Bruno behind the ears.

Piper smiled back. 'Just wait until I bring the hamsters out.'

And this time, Kara actually laughed. She may have even snorted a bit. She tucked up her legs so there was room for Piper to sit on the couch. As she sat, Piper felt something small and hard behind her. She reached back and pulled out a mini vodka bottle. Fishing around in the crevices of the couch, she found a half-sized bottle of red. A half-sized bottle of white. Unzipping a bulging cushion cover, she discovered two mini scotches and a half-sized bottle of champagne. All empty. Kara stared at her as she placed each bottle on the floor in front of them.

'And that was just for breakfast,' Kara said, her eyes rolling back in her head.

Piper grimaced. Even though Kara's speech was pretty good, that sort of eye-rolling made it clear she was still far from sober. It was the hazy, out-of-control look Dylan would get sometimes when he got too stoned. She would be trying to talk to him about something. Friends, plans, anything. He'd be fine for a while. Then his responses would become agonisingly slow. Occasionally, he'd snap back to attention like Kara seemed to do when Bruno snorted, but then he'd sink back. Then the eye-rolling.

As soon as the eye-rolling happened, Piper knew there was no point trying to have a conversation with him. The few times Piper had smoked with him, she hadn't enjoyed her disjointed thoughts and that feeling of losing touch with reality, but Dylan often seemed hell-bent on going to La La Land. Piper would try to bring him back with cold face washers and iced water drinks, or she'd let him sleep it off.

But she didn't think Vivian would be overly impressed with the sleep-it-off approach, so she decided on the former.

She walked from the lounge room to the bedroom and found the spacious marble bathroom. It was full of fluffy white towels and face washers. Piper wet some and took them back to the couch. She lay the washer over Kara's forehead and the towel over her chest. Kara relaxed for a moment, and then she sat up.

'If you have to report back, that's okay,' she said slowly. Piper had the sense that she was trying hard to speak clearly. To sound more sober than she was. There was such a big gap between Kara's words that Piper had to think hard to string them together.

'But make sure you tell them,' Kara continued, 'that Larry diden... din't... did not know anything about it. I told him the bar fridge was empty and he believed me. I did most of the drinking before he even got here. Then when he got here, I poured the booze in ... into my teacup.'

Piper tilted her head. 'I can't believe you can even talk,' she said, feeling a bit guilty at the image of a very out-of-it Dylan coming into her mind. 'God, are you okay?'

Kara drew her legs to her chest and tucked her arms around them. 'Experience, I guess. I'm piss fit. Another thing to be proud of, don't you think?'

Piper shrugged. Obviously, it wasn't ideal to be in the process of sobering up before midday. And being *piss fit*, as Kara called it, seemed to suggest that her problems with alcohol were bigger than a one-off breakfast binge. But Piper wasn't going to judge her. Kara was doing enough of that without her help.

Piper sighed. 'I'll just grab you a big glass of water and we can —'

'I bet you think I'm a self-obsessed, self-indulgent twat,' Kara interrupted her, still talking slowly, but with determination. 'Most people prob'ly think that when I get wasted ... *poor little rich girl. The supermodel who has everything and it's not enough.* Is that what you think?'

The gaps between her words were closing up a bit, as though she was *actually* getting more sober now and not play-acting at being sober.

'Well,' Piper said, collecting her thoughts. She knew that people tended to get more upset about stuff when they were drunk; things got blown out of proportion. Still, whichever way she looked at it, Kara seemed to be really down on herself. Piper searched her mind for something to say. 'I kind of feel that if you're judging *yourself* as self-indulgent and self-obsessed,' she said, thinking the gap-between-words-thing must have been contagious because Piper was doing it herself now, trying to pick the right words, 'then it's probably not the case. Since you can obviously stand outside yourself for long enough to consider how other people may see you. And your concern about dumping Larry in it also suggests that your level of *twattiness* could be much lower than you think.'

Kara covered her mouth with both hands. For a terrible moment, Piper thought she was about to cry. But Kara wasn't crying. In fact, she was biting down on a smile, even though her eyes still glistened from leftover tears.

'*Twattiness*, hey?' she said. 'That's pretty original. For a self-helpy rant.'

Piper smiled back. 'Ah well, it was off the cuff. If I had more time to prepare, it would be awesome.'

'I'll *never* drink again,' Kara joked. 'Want to have a water or two with me?'

'I haven't seen you at *Aspire* before,' Kara said suddenly. Quite a few glasses of water later, they were sitting on the plush Persian carpet in the middle of the lounge room, chatting and playing with Bruno.

'No, well . . . today is kind of my first day,' admitted Piper.

Kara looked surprised. 'Really?'

'Yeah. I just moved here from Mission Beach,' Piper offered. 'I've lived there all my life. I just came to Melbourne for this job.'

'Where's Mission Beach?'

'It's up north. Near Cairns.'

'Yes!' Kara cried, snapping her fingers. 'I did a shoot up there once. It was so relaxed and friendly. Everyone in the town knew everyone else.'

'Yes, that's pretty much it.'

'I came from a country town, too,' Kara said. 'But I moved away when I was "discovered" at fourteen, and I've been working ever since. Modelling is it, for me. It's all I've ever known.'

'Living the dream, hey?' Piper said teasingly.

Kara blew out a breath. 'Yeah, right,' she said. 'Or surviving the nightmare. I've given *everything* to get where I am. And I'm starting to think it's too much.' She pointed to the tabloid that was still on the couch. 'It's not just stuff like that,' she said softly. 'It's more like. . . ' she paused, as though looking for the right words. 'You can't be *real* in this industry. I've got to hide the

44

parts of myself that don't fit in with the Kara Kingston Marketing Machine.'

Piper nodded, but she wasn't exactly sure what Kara meant about hiding parts of herself. Maybe the partying had something to do with it.

Or maybe Kara is just in a bad place because her boyfriend is an arrogant know-it-all? Piper mused. Maybe she needed to break up with Mason, if he was causing her so much pain. Whatever it was, Kara looked totally exhausted.

'Do you want me to get a blanket?' Larry asked, coming back into the suite.

Piper nodded. It was weird to be the one giving directions.

Kara leaned over and pulled the tabloid towards her. 'I need them,' she said, looking at the picture. 'I need them both.'

Piper frowned. She had no idea what Kara was talking about now. She needed the alcohol? The alcohol *and* Mason? *What she probably needs*, Piper thought, *is to tell Mason to stop treating her like shit.*

Larry handed Piper a soft, cream cashmere blanket, which she drew over Kara.

'How about another cup of tea, love?' Larry asked.

⁓

When Kara's agent, Anita Barnes, strode into the room an hour or so later, the atmosphere shifted.

The woman was so botoxed that not a wrinkle remained on her face, even though it was obvious that she was well into her fifties. But she must have been due for a collagen shot in her lips, which were thin, with heavy lipliner drawn way outside the boundaries of her actual mouth. Her hair fell around her waxy face in thick stripes of black and silver. *Cruella Deville*, Piper thought to herself.

'Jesus, Larry. What the fuck kind of army were you in? The bloody boy scouts?' Anita demanded. Without waiting for an answer, she strode over and ripped the blanket off Kara. 'And what are you doing here?' she spat at Piper.

Piper got up from the floor. 'I'm from *Aspire*,' she said, trying to sound confident. 'I'm helping.'

'Then *help*,' Anita barked. 'Run the shower. Cold water. Now.'

'Kara's okay now. She's just resting,' Larry said falteringly. 'She's had a bit of a hard morning.'

'Well, it just got harder,' Anita snapped, pulling a dozy Kara up to stand. Piper noticed that, despite the fact that she was speaking okay, Kara was definitely still wobbly on her feet. 'Larry, get her in the shower. Make sure it's cold.'

Piper saw Larry's grimace. Anita must have picked up on it too. 'Hair and make-up will be here in half an hour, and we have to at least give them something *hygienic* to work with.' She turned an accusing look at Kara.

'You look like shit,' she said. 'Go fix yourself up.' She turned back to Larry. 'Jesus, Larry, she'll need some support.' She gave

Piper a dismissive glance. 'As in, more support than this chihuahua could give her. And it's not like Kara has anything the world hasn't seen already.'

Larry walked over. He placed his arm around Kara's shoulder and under her arm to steady her. 'Okay love, let's walk,' he said, his kindness all the more noticeable after Anita's tirade.

Piper went ahead and ran the shower. At the last moment, she added a bit of hot water, hoping no-one would notice.

Kara submitted meekly, with Larry holding her. As she disrobed, Piper almost gasped. God, her body was impossible. Her breasts were round and full. Her waist was narrow, and her legs seemed to go forever. She was a freak of nature.

Although Kara didn't seem to care that she was naked in front of him, Larry turned the other way.

Piper sighed. She couldn't believe this was Kara Kingston, who had it all. Kara Kingston, who was rich and beautiful, was clearly in pain. Despite the fact that Kara was a few years older, a few heads taller and about a thousand times more successful, Piper felt protective of her.

'Girl!' Anita's voice bulleted its way into the bathroom. Piper, assuming the *girl* was her, checked with Larry that Kara was okay to be left in the shower and walked back into the lounge room. Anita was on the phone. She paused, putting a hand over the phone. 'Did she say anything?'

'Um,' Piper said, 'I think she was a bit upset about the article in the paper.'

Anita grabbed the paper from the couch, took it into the kitchen and stuffed it into the bin. In ten seconds, she was back. She narrowed her eyes and stared at Piper through the slits. *'Anything else?'*

Piper felt like she was being interrogated. She had no idea what Anita was getting at but even if Piper knew something, she wasn't sure she'd tell this woman.

'Not a thing,' she said.

Anita nodded. 'Good.' Her face relaxed as much as it could, given the botox. 'All right. I've got her now. You can go. And take that animal with you,' she said, nodding at Bruno, who was lying in the middle of the floor snoring contentedly.

Piper woke Bruno and put him into her bag. As she walked out the door, she heard Anita on the phone.

'No, Mason. I really think it's the right thing.'

There was a pause. Piper lingered in the doorway, wanting to hear what they were talking about. *Hasn't Mason already done enough damage?* she thought to herself.

'Of course I'm sure,' Anita continued. 'I've managed her career for seven years now. I've got her to the top. That's where she's going to stay, Mason.' There was another pause. 'You and her, it's *imperative ...'*

Just then, Anita looked up. She gave Piper a glare from hell, and Piper shot out into the foyer, shutting the door behind her.

On the way back to the office, Piper spotted an ice-cream shop, and decided she deserved a little pick-me-up after dealing with Kara and Anita all afternoon. A cheeky double cone that she could eat on the sunny riverbank was just the thing.

5

Coffee. Mason needed coffee. Of course, he could have sent someone to go and fetch a double-shot latte for him, but it wouldn't have been enough. What he needed was a coffee *break*.

He kept looking straight ahead as he walked down the boulevard. There was always the chance of running into someone from the office, and he desperately wanted to minimise that risk.

Mason detoured to give Cafe Condor a wide berth. Ducking down a narrow lane, he already felt himself breathing easier. Passing Cafe Condor was a major danger. People who wanted to be *seen* spent copious amounts of time there. People who would suck up to Mason's dad, Patrick Wakefield, like he was the second coming, just to get an in with the mag. In the absence of his father,

Mason would be their target. Mason had grown up with all that bullshit. That was one of the reasons why he'd escaped.

O'Dwyer's was one of the few good things about having to come back to Melbourne. It was a bar more than a cafe, but it opened mid-morning and the coffee was great. Mason liked the pool table with the green lampshades hanging overhead, the dark wooden bar stools, the music — usually Sinatra, Etta James or Billie Holiday — playing softly.

As soon as Mason took a seat on a bar stool, the owner, Sam, set to work making Mason's usual double-shot latte.

'How are you?' asked Sam, a slinging a checked tea towel over his shoulder.

'I'm —' Mason didn't even get to the second word of his sentence before his phone buzzed. Caller ID told him it was Rufus Ellington, chairman of the board. As much as he needed a break, he knew he had to answer the call.

'Are you prepared for the board meeting on Thursday?' Typical Rufus Ellington: no pleasantries. 'We'll need to see *Aspire's* financial situation clearly. If the numbers don't add up, we're not going to be able to get that loan. Got it?'

'I've got it, Rufus,' Mason replied. Christ, there would be hours of work in getting that all ready. Mason could kiss sleep goodbye for the next few nights.

'Mason,' Rufus added gruffly, 'things can't continue as they were under your father. As well as the internal changes you're implementing, we'd like to see a new direction for the magazine.

The circulation figures are a disgrace.'

Mason exhaled loudly as he hung up. *A new direction. Jesus.* He knew his father and Rose had been discussing some changes and analysing possible market responses to different ideas before his dad went off the rails. While he was in the States he'd had several emails from his father, musing on the best ways to change things around. Several ideas had been floated between Rose and Patrick, ranging from expanding *Aspire*'s online presence to seeking out freelance feature writers and having in-house writers change their approach to developing articles.

But from where Mason stood, it all seemed risky. At a time when mag sales were getting tougher and tougher, the last thing they needed to do was alienate their existing readers. It was a difficult call to make. Especially for an acting CEO. And Mason certainly felt like he'd been *acting* since he'd been pulled into *Aspire*. He practically deserved an Oscar.

His phone buzzed again, interrupting his thoughts. This time it was a blocked number. He'd learned not to answer those calls out of the office. It was never good news.

Sam put the coffee down on the bar in front of Mason as the phone went on buzzing between them.

'Sorry, what was your question, Sam?' asked Mason.

'Well, it was going to be a simple *how are you*,' Sam joked. 'But I think I'll pass on the answer.' He wiped the bar with his tea towel. 'All work, no play and all that,' Sam advised.

Mason shook his head. 'Pot, kettle and all that,' he fired back.

Sam flicked the tea towel at him.

'I guess it's just the way it is, Sam,' Mason said. 'Until Dad comes back, at least.'

'How is he?' Sam asked.

Mason took a sip of his coffee. 'He's not good. He spends most of his time lying on the couch.'

'What's the latest on his ex-wife?'

Mason felt his hackles rising at the mention of Abigail, who had walked into Patrick's life six years ago. She'd always been on the nose. For starters, she was only a few years older than Mason and he had seen the dollar signs in her eyes from the get-go. Patrick had been smitten, though, for the first time since Mason's mum had died, eight years earlier. Mason could see that.

But at the time, Mason had been desperate to go to New York. Desperate to start a life out from under the shadow of his media-mogul father. Before he'd left for Harvard, the only thing he'd asked of Patrick was that he get a pre-nup before marrying Abigail. The request had created a rift between Mason and Patrick, who refused to believe Abigail was only interested in his money.

But now, Abigail had manoeuvred her way into a new relationship with another older man. *Coincidentally* one who'd made it onto *Forbes'* rich list. Without a pre-nup, Patrick stood to lose a lot.

'The court date is set for next month,' Mason said. 'I just hope Dad's better by then. Between that and the magazine going backwards ...' he trailed off.

Sam leant towards him. 'You're doing a good thing,' he said. 'Just out of Harvard, with your MBA and the world at your feet. It's a big thing for you to pause for your dad's sake. But you're young, you've got lots of time. And sometimes, life's detours take you somewhere special.'

Mason attempted a smile. Sam might have been right about some of life's detours. But not this one. Taking over at *Aspire* had never been on his radar. He wanted to make it alone; he didn't want to follow in his dad's footsteps. He'd even had a job offer in Silicon Valley after finishing his MBA. It had been an amazing opportunity, but one he couldn't accept.

Rose had tried to battle it out alone after Abigail had left and his father went downhill. But it was too much for her to implement any major changes without Patrick there. Despite her best efforts, things had unravelled at *Aspire*, and she'd finally had no choice but to ask Mason to come back and step into Patrick's shoes. Mason couldn't just stand back and let everything his dad had worked for go down the gurgler.

Mason thought he could help, but at times felt out of his depth. He could see, in a strict business sense, what had to be done: old extravagances needed to go and any dead wood cut away. But it was a tough gig. And being under pressure to make major decisions about a new direction for the mag was nerve wracking. His dad's shoes sometimes felt like a giant's.

'They all hate me in there, Sam,' Mason said. 'I'm their worst nightmare.'

'You're not there to make friends. And people always dislike change,' Sam said reassuringly. He held his left hand out. 'Business,' he said, making a fist. Then his right hand shot out. 'Friends,' he continued. 'No need to mix them up.'

Mason checked his phone. God, he'd been here for forty-five minutes. Forty-five minutes he didn't have.

He took a deep breath and started mentally prioritising the million things on his to-do list. He had a meeting with the head of advertising at 11 a.m. Then prep for the board meeting. With all the recent staff cuts, he didn't even have an assistant. He'd have to ask Rose to lend him someone to help with the figures tomorrow. Jesus. And a direction to secure a new readership? He knew about business strategy, but he knew very little about how to increase a dying magazine's circulation.

He had a sudden urge to talk to Kara. She was a gem for stepping into the Dinnigan shoot at such late notice. *Aspire* was very lucky to have her on board – and for less than half the fee she normally charged. Her agent would probably have her head for this. Or his.

Mason's finger hovered over her name in his address book, then he shook his head. The last thing Kara needed was him crying on her shoulder. She had her own problems. She hadn't been good the other weekend.

Kara had been fragile for years, but Mason was surprised at how dependent on alcohol she'd become in his time away. He didn't know how to handle the situation — he knew just being there for her wasn't enough. But right now, even *that* was more than he could manage.

⁓

That afternoon, Mason looked up from the figures on his screen and gazed out the meeting-room window, to where the river sparkled in the sun.

A silver flash on the riverside caught his eye. He saw it was Rose's little pug in his silver jacket, leaping up and down. With Bruno was the girl — the one who had bumped into him this morning. He could hardly believe what he saw in her hand: a double ice-cream cone.

It had been a long time since Mason had witnessed a woman eating ice-cream, let alone a double cone. Usually it was a salad with no dressing, and Mason had noticed how even that usually got pushed around plates rather than actually being eaten.

The dog was using his best leaping techniques on the girl, with a spin at the top of each leap. People on the riverbank looked at the girl and the dog, but she seemed completely unaware of the attention — which was unusual too. Most girls Mason knew were acutely aware of their assets, ready to hawk them for whatever they were worth.

He watched as the girl took a huge, indelicate bite of the ice-cream, then held a finger up to Bruno, telling him to wait. Her long hair caught the sunlight, and she casually scooped it up and pushed it to the side, exposing the long, delicate curve of her neck.

Something stirred inside Mason at the sight of her bare neck. He watched, transfixed, as she gave the last of the ice-cream to the pug.

Focus, Wakefield. He checked himself. What was he doing, staring out the window at some junior? He needed to stay focused. That was how he'd gotten through his MBA, and it was what he had to do now. If he didn't pull his shit together, this magazine was going to collapse.

6

'Well, how was it, my darling girl?' Gaynor asked. She muted the huge flat screen TV and picked up her champagne glass.

Piper tried to describe her day. Luckily Gaynor was a good listener. Piper worked backwards, from the tasks Vivian had given her when she got back to *Aspire* after the Langham. That part had been good, actually – just sitting at her computer and filling in stock orders for an upcoming shoot. She'd needed something simple and straightforward like that. Then she gave a brief account of the Kara debacle, and then, finally, Mason's appearance in the office that morning.

Piper wasn't sure why, but she left out the bit about overhearing Anita on the phone to Mason. Probably because she wanted to get the facts straight before she said anything about what she'd heard.

But it also was more than that, somehow. Something Piper didn't want to admit, even to herself.

All she knew was that the idea of Mason dating Kara and breaking her heart rankled on a number of levels.

'I've met Mason Wakefield a number of times,' Gaynor remarked.

The mention of his name gave Piper a shock. Like Gaynor had read her mind. Piper bit her lip and waited while Gaynor poured herself another glass of champagne and took a sip. It seemed to take a long time.

'He's a lovely young man,' Gaynor continued.

'Lovely?' Piper said. That was definitely not the word that sprung to mind when she thought about him. Handsome, yes. Intimidating, yes. Arrogant, yes. But not *lovely*.

'Yes, lovely,' Gaynor confirmed. 'I knew his mother, too. She was an amazing woman. Died of cancer, at least fourteen years ago now. Poor Mason was only a boy. It must have been so hard for him.'

A shiver ran down Piper's spine. As much as her mum had been annoying and judgemental about her relationship with Dylan, the thought of losing her was too hideous to contemplate.

It was impossible to imagine her self-assured boss, the man who broke Kara Kingston's heart, as a vulnerable kid who'd lost his mum. *Maybe that's what makes him so difficult*, thought Piper. *Or maybe*, she told herself sternly, *I'm just reading too much into everything again.*

'What did *you* think of Mason?' Gaynor asked, cutting across her thoughts.

Piper shrugged, as though he hadn't made any big impression. 'He seemed all right,' she said noncommittally. It was time to steer the conversation away from Mason Wakefield. 'So, Gaynes, what did you get up to today?'

Gaynor stretched and walked to the kitchen. Piper wished she wasn't hearing the tinkle of Gaynor's champagne glass being refilled. At least she normally waited until 5 p.m. to pour her first drink, unlike Kara Kingston. But it seemed she'd keep on going until bedtime. Her godmother was definitely drinking too much.

'I had a lunch date!' Gaynor said, coming back into the lounge room and taking her place on the couch again. Piper felt her tone was wrong. A tad too theatrical, even for Gaynor.

'Cool,' Piper said. 'How did it go?'

'Yes. Good,' Gaynor chirped. 'Well, fine.' Her next go at the champagne was more of a slug than a sip.

'Okay, from the beginning, please.'

Gaynor smiled. 'It's so nice to have you here, Piper,' she said, trying to change the subject.

'And?' Piper giggled, not letting her get away with it.

'Well, we met online,' Gaynor sighed, giving in. 'His name was Ron.' Piper noticed Gaynor's use of the past tense, but didn't say anything.

'I was very impressed by the restaurant he chose,' Gaynor continued. 'It was quite stunning. I'll take you there sometime, Piper.

It was all white tablecloths and waiters in bow ties. Huge flower arrangements. Truly elegant. He was there when I arrived. Quite a nice-looking man, around my age. Quite cultured too. We had. . . well. . . I *thought* we had a lovely chat about a play we'd both seen.' Piper couldn't help noticing a little sigh before Gaynor resumed her tale. 'He had the ocean trout and I had a lemon-tarragon lobster roll, which was lovely.'

'Gaynes, that's great,' Piper said encouragingly. There was definitely something odd in the way Gaynor was phrasing things, though. 'Where's the *but*?'

Gaynor shook her head. 'There was a little glitch at the end,' she said with a shrug. Piper's heart sank.

'A little glitch or a glitch with a capital G?'

Gaynor rolled her eyes. 'Well, when the bill came, the waiter put it in front of Ron,' she said. 'And Ron immediately pushed it over to me. Then he said . . . ' Gaynor's voice transformed, so she sounded just like a man. '*It's been lovely to meet you, Gaynor. Of course, you will understand that I'm looking for someone quite a bit younger than yourself. But I do wish you luck in your endeavours.*'

'Oh my god,' Piper cried. 'Bastard! But I'm sure *you will understand* that Ron is a loser. With a capital L. I'm sorry, Gaynes.'

Gaynor downed the rest of her champagne. 'No matter,' she said. 'I'm a trouper, don't forget.' When she stood up again, Gaynor was unsteady on her feet. 'There's always tomorrow, Piper,' she said majestically. 'Goodnight, darling.'

Piper put on her pyjamas, fluffed the pillows and sat back in bed with her phone. Gaynor's bad date swirled around in her head, along with all the other things that had happened that day. What she needed was to speak with her boyfriend.

She scrolled to a picture of Dylan on her phone. Classic Dylan, in his navy singlet and work overalls, standing in the frame of a half-built block of flats. His hair was sandy and sun-bleached from surfing. He was waving to the camera, grinning. God, she missed those muscular arms holding her. Those hands. Her skin tingled as she thought about what those hands had done for her. She dialled his number.

'Piper? Hey hon. How's my best . . . hey, turn it down, can ya, Loftie?' There was a little scuttle in the background and then the volume of the music in the background went down.

'How's my best girl?' Dylan asked.

'I'm fine. I think,' Piper said. 'Where are you?'

'Just home with the boys,' Dylan said. His voice was languid and thick.

'Getting stoned?' Piper asked. She felt a niggling sense of annoyance, and made a mental note to call him earlier in the evenings in future. He sounded okay, not really high, but she knew he was somewhere on the way. He normally didn't smoke on Monday nights. It would've been good to have a proper conversation with him.

'Yeah, no, just a few cones, a couple of beers. That's all, babe.'

Piper sighed quietly to herself. She would have to talk about it with him sometime. Dylan worked really hard, and smoking was his way of relaxing. But it was getting too full on. Right now wasn't the time to talk about it, though. Not on the phone, while they were both adjusting to being apart.

'Who's there, Dyl?' she asked, her voice even.

'Ah, you know. Loftie. Animal. The usual suspects.' He paused. Someone laughed in the background. 'Hang on,' he said, 'I'm gonna take you somewhere private.'

Piper smiled. She could imagine Dylan traipsing through the flat, trying to find a place to sit that wasn't occupied by empty pizza boxes and beer cans. Loftie and Dylan's flat might be a bit 'junky', like her mum said after picking her up from there once, but those guys did pretty well for themselves as far as Piper was concerned. If her mum just got to know him a bit better, gave him a chance, she'd see that Dylan was mature in a lot of ways. He worked. He paid his own rent, his own bills, with no help from his parents. He was totally independent. Not many of Piper's friends could say the same.

'Orright, got you,' Dylan said finally.

'Where are you?'

'In the loo,' Dylan laughed. 'The quietest place I could find.'

'Nice,' Piper laughed. It was so weird to think of him in there, especially after today. On the bathroom door, Piper knew, was a *Sports Illustrated* poster of Kara Kingston in a skimpy yellow bikini.

'Miss you already, babe,' Dylan said. 'How was your first day?'

'Pretty good,' Piper said. She wanted to tell Dylan what had happened, but she could tell he wouldn't really follow it all right now. She could catch him up another time. Anyway, she was practically talked-out after her chat with Gaynor. 'See that model in the yellow bikini on the loo door?' she asked instead. She couldn't resist.

'What, Kara Kingston?'

'I met her today.'

'No way!' Dylan shouted, sounding like he'd snapped out of his stoned state and was listening properly. 'Jesus, she's . . . man, she's . . .'

'I know,' Piper agreed. She couldn't blame him. If there was a litmus test for hetero males, Kara Kingston was it.

'But she's not as hot as you, babe,' Dylan said quickly. Piper smiled. She really had to stop testing Dylan. He didn't deserve it. He'd never given her any reason to feel insecure, but she still did sometimes.

'Thanks, Dyl.'

'It's true, babe. So, you reckon it's a goer? The job?'

'I think so. It's too early to tell, really. But I miss you. Have you booked a plane ticket yet?'

'I'm onto it this week,' Dylan said. 'Promise. So, where are you right now?'

'In my new bedroom,' Piper said.

'Mmmm, what's it like?'

'I've got a king-sized bed. Amazing sheets. Mirrors.'

'Oh my god, you're killing me. I'll book the tickets tomorrow. Hang on, sweet.' Piper waited. Dylan must have gone back into the lounge room. The music had been turned up again.

'Is that Beyoncé?' Piper asked. Loftie usually controlled the iPod at the boys' place, and he was definitely not a Beyoncé kind of guy.

'It's the radio,' Dylan said. 'Anyway, sweet, I'm feeling pretty chillaxed. Going to go and get some z's. 'Night.'

Piper frowned. Dylan seemed to be in a hurry to hang up. But then again, it was pretty late, and Dylan's workday started at 6 a.m.

'Love you,' she said.

'Love you more,' Dylan cooed.

A warm feeling washed over her at his familiar reply. She hung up the phone, turned the lamp off and settled herself in the giant bed. She really had to take a leaf out of Dylan's book. Get chillaxed. She was probably overstimulated because of her weird first day at work.

She let herself drift, thinking of Dylan's arms around her. She was so lucky to have him in her life.

Love you more.

And then she slept. Like a babe.

7

The three receptionists looked just as exquisite on Tuesday morning as they had the day before. In fact, it seemed to Piper that they'd taken glamour to new, soaring heights. Underneath the desk, Piper spied three pairs of killer-high black stilettos that she wouldn't have even been able to stand in, let alone walk. *But then again*, Piper reassured herself, looking down at her grey pinstripe skirt and red Mary Janes, *they probably don't have to get around the building very much.*

On the plasma screen behind them, a funny-looking older man with white hair and big black sunglasses was being interviewed.

'Karl Lagerfield,' Piper said aloud, quite proud that she recognised the designer.

The black-haired receptionist looked at Piper with raised

eyebrows. 'Karl Lager*feld*,' she corrected, running her hand over the silver lapels of her black jacket.

It was too good an opportunity to resist. 'Best and Less,' Piper joked, running her hands down her own outfit.

The receptionist's face broke into a grin as she answered her next call. It made her look human.

'Hello, *Angela* speaking,' she said into the phone, making eye contact with Piper as she said her name, by way of introduction. Piper waved. Walking towards her office and dodging the hallway scrum with a bit more grace than the day before, she felt like she'd cracked the code, or at least part of it. It was a good feeling to know that there was a way to break down barriers with most people — you just had to figure out what it was.

When Piper reached the fashion department, Vivian and Lucy were already there. Vivian was looking over Lucy's shoulder, pointing something out on her computer. In a sequinned black singlet, a skin-tight red pencil skirt that came to her knees and black patent leather pumps, Vivian looked as formidable as ever.

'Morning, Lucy, morning, Viv,' Piper said.

Vivian turned around and gave Piper one of her dagger looks. Behind Vivian's back, Lucy screwed up her face. She held her index fingers together and drew them apart, nodding at Piper like she was doing a charade that told Piper to extend a certain word.

'Ah, I mean, morning, *Vivian*,' Piper said, hoping she'd interpreted Lucy's gesture correctly. Vivian dimmed her glare just a little. Apparently Rose was allowed to shorten Vivian's name, but that right didn't extend to Piper. God, Piper was glad Lucy was around to give her the heads up. She had a very strong feeling that Vivian might be an exception; there might not be any way to break down *her* barrier.

Just then, Bronwyn appeared at the doorway, struggling her way around a stack of prop boxes that had been parked in the middle of the bustling hallway. She was wearing an unusual red linen dress with a drop waist that seemed to have a bit of the Japanese influence Bronwyn apparently liked to thread through her clothes. Lucy had told Piper how keen Bronwyn was to talk to Vivian about her creations but, so far, she hadn't built up the courage. Which wasn't a wonder. No matter how many times she'd been told, Vivian refused to even use the intern's name. Without even turning around, Vivian clicked her fingers over her shoulder and barked at her. 'Coffee.' Even under the shoulder pads, Piper could see Bronwyn's shoulders sag as she backed away.

'Today I want you,' Vivian said, clicking her manicured fingers at Piper, 'to research and collate which celebrities have jumped on the sheer bandwagon in any couture label in the past three months. I want dates, events, locations. You have until noon. Got it?'

Piper nodded, trying to look serious and sure of herself. She had no idea what a *sheer bandwagon* was, but she wasn't going to admit that aloud.

Vivian picked up a stack of mags from Lucy's desk and started striding out of the office. 'Sheer panels,' she called out over her shoulder as she walked out.

Piper was enjoying this. It felt more like play than work. Sheer panels, she discovered, were replacing whole sections of dresses, with the wearer going commando underneath. Gwyneth Paltrow and J. Lo had pulled this look off super successfully. There was also a development on this trend, where whole dresses were sheer, and any underwear was completely visible. Piper had fun getting information about who was wearing the dresses, and when. On her computer screen at the moment were Jennifer Lawrence and Selena Gomez, both rocking sheer dresses with completely visible lingerie. Piper checked the clock. She still had an hour and a half before Vivian would return to the office. Lucy had hurried off on some errand, so, aside from the constant trickle of people going to and from the fashion cupboard, she was alone.

Piper looked at Jennifer Lawrence in the sheer Dior gown. Perhaps it was her role in the tough world of *The Hunger Games* that made Piper wonder about the origin of the trend. Why were so many women baring all these days? Piper remembered reading about the 'Lipstick effect' theory: apparently, in an economic downturn, women will buy more luxury items like lipstick, and bare more flesh, partly to cheer themselves up but also to attract men. Could the lipstick effect be applied to the sheer dress trend? Times were certainly tough economically.

In a sudden burst of inspiration, Piper wrote a short piece about the lipstick effect and fashion. She knew she was supposed to be researching, not writing, but there was something satisfying about using her research to write a piece on how the theory was relevant to this modern trend. When she'd finished, she added the title 'Sheer Sense'. She felt a bit like she'd finished a jigsaw puzzle, and was happy with how she'd fitted things together. Of course, it was just a quick little writing experiment; she wouldn't show it to anyone. As soon as Vivian came back, Piper could just switch screens back to the results of her research.

'Sheer Sense, huh?'

Piper turned around. She'd been so engrossed, and had become so used to the constant hum of action from the hallway, that she hadn't heard Vivian come into the office. Now, Vivian was standing right behind her, scanning the article over her shoulder. Piper braced herself for a dressing down, but she secretly hoped Vivian might be pleased with her initiative. She even allowed a tiny snippet of daydream that Vivian might even include grabs from the article in the fashion pages.

'Well,' Vivian sneered. 'How very ambitious of you, Piper. Gosh, let's publish it straightaway! We have a *journalist* on our hands. Let's see what you've done.' Piper was silent as Vivian kept reading the article. 'This is all right,' she finally announced. 'As in, not a complete disaster.'

Piper looked at her. She almost detected a twitch at the sides of Vivian's mouth, as though she might be a tiny bit pleased. But, very soon, the old Vivian was back in full force. 'So, did you actually do what I asked? Or did you just go off on your own tangent?'

If she was trying to stamp out any remnant of Piper's crazy hope, she'd succeeded. Piper turned to her computer, clicked out of the 'Sheer Sense' screen and returned to the research, scrolling through all the information and images she'd found.

'Piper,' Vivian clicked her fingers and pointed up the corridor. 'You need to get up to Rose's office. She wants to see you.'

Piper bit her lip. The finger clicking was driving her nuts. Even if she was a dogsbody, she wasn't a dog! Bronwyn seemed to have decided there was nothing she could do about it, but that wasn't Piper's nature. She had to say something.

'Okay, Vivian,' she said carefully, 'but is it possible for you to stop clicking your fingers at me?'

Vivian tilted her head and narrowed her eyes. 'Don't get ahead of yourself.'

⁓

As she walked towards Rose's office, skirting around a group of half-naked models in huge, frizzy, white-blonde wigs, Piper took some deep, calming breaths. Vivian was just a bitch — it was no big deal. It gave Piper a little pleasure, at least, to indulge in a fantasy. She imagined herself walking into Rose's office with a print-out of the 'Sheer Sense' article.

Rose would read it straightaway. She would comment on Piper's writing style and the interesting angle she'd taken. 'Please,' Rose would say, 'would you mind moving to features? We need you. Bust out. Do something bigger, something more ambitious. It's clear you can handle it, with your talent.'

Then Piper would write a feature article. She wasn't sure what it would be about yet, but something would occur to her. Something fascinating that they couldn't refuse to publish. Something that would win a coveted Australian Publishers Excellence Award. Something that would stick it right up finger-clicking Vivian.

Piper arrived outside Rose's office, and looked through the glass door. Rose was wearing blue culottes and a cream silk shirt. As she moved around the office, phone in one hand, Piper was reminded of a cloud in the sky. Rose turned Piper's way and waved her in with her free hand, motioning towards a guest chair.

As soon as Piper sat down, the fantasy evaporated. Rose may have been floaty, but she was also clearly super busy.

'Yes, I've seen your spring range, Donatella,' Rose said into the phone. 'It's perfect. There isn't a piece I wouldn't want to use.'

Rose was on the phone to *Donatella Versace*. Even if Piper did have the guts to show Rose her article, she was pretty sure that reading it wouldn't be high on Rose's priority list.

'Yes, but of course we have Kit Willow's spring range too. I think a bit of mix-and-match would give the best results. The romance of the eclectic, you know?' There was a pause. 'Lovely to speak with you too, Donatella.'

Rose hung up the phone and looked at Piper. She sat down, pouring two cups of tea from the large silver teapot in front of her. She put one in front of Piper.

'It's camomile,' she said, 'to soothe nerves and restore balance.'

Piper took a sip and tried to imagine the tea soothing and balancing her. Rose leant back in her chair and fluffed her blonde curls. Before Piper could speak, there was a knock at the door.

'Come in,' Rose called. 'Piper, this is Wendy Roberts. She and Lawrence Sharp form the team over at features.'

Piper took in a breath. She tried not to stare, but it *was* interesting to meet someone who wrote features articles for a living. Wendy was glamorous, but in a different way to most people Piper had met at the *Aspire* offices. Her dark hair was cut into a geometrical bob and she wore a black dress and grey ballet flats. Piper thought she looked intelligent, though that could have been something to do with her red Prada glasses. For some reason they were perched on the tip of her nose.

'So, we're a hundred per cent sure we're going to go with "Thinking Threesome"?' Wendy asked Rose. Although she'd nodded politely at Piper, it was clear Wendy was preoccupied. 'Because I'm just touching up an alternative and I think I could finish it by the time we go to press.' Now it occurred to Piper why Wendy's glasses might be perched on the end of her nose. Wendy probably only wore them for reading and writing, and that, if Rose gave the okay, she would be back in her office and onto her computer within seconds.

'It still goes into the whole *idea* of group sex,' she continued, passion in her voice, 'but it just goes a bit deeper into the psychological repercussions. I've been able to access amazing reports. If we just up the word count to two thousand . . .' Wendy stopped mid-sentence, responding to the look on Rose's face.

'Sorry, Wendy,' Rose said. 'We're staying with the status quo at the moment until we make some decisions about the new direction. We're discussing strategies and looking into different models. But keep it light for the time being, okay?'

The sense of urgency Piper had felt before fizzled. God, if she had more experience, if she'd been asked, she would have loved to join the conversation. She'd come across stuff about threesomes in magazines sometimes. Usually, they were pretty ludicrous — just designed to titillate. But to *really* investigate how things worked in a situation most people would never experience for themselves . . . less as far as she was concerned, Wendy's idea sounded fascinating.

Wendy took off her glasses. 'Yes, of course, Rose. Understood,' she said with a tight smile. Then she left the office.

Piper wished she could follow her back to the features department to pick her brains about writing, but Vivian's warning not to get ahead of herself still rang in her head.

Rose took a sip of her camomile tea and her phone rang. She checked caller ID.

'Ah, something else to soothe the nerves,' she said with a smile before answering the phone. 'Mason. How are things up in the turret?' Piper heard the warm tone in Rose's voice. She was surprised that Rose would refer to Mason as someone who soothed nerves. In Piper's experience, he was more likely to fray them.

Whatever Mason said at the other end made Rose chuckle. Piper got up to go, but Rose motioned for her to sit back down.

'Oh, Mason,' said Rose. 'That is a big job, and of course you can't do it alone. I know you don't have a PA since we let Petra go, but we can at least get someone up to help. The boardroom is currently being used by the art department, but it's free at four and you'll be able to spread out there. I'll send someone up to meet you there. Anything else?'

Rose nodded at Piper, indicating that *she* was the someone who was being sent up to meet Mason Wakefield. Her heart started to beat faster. God, was she really going to be working with Mason Wakefield? The idea was pretty scary.

Now, Piper felt herself straining to hear what Mason was saying on the other end of the phone. Rose's laugh tinkled around her office and Piper felt confused. Was Mason making a joke? Was he actually a nice guy?

Rose was still smiling when she put down the phone. 'Piper, I did have other plans for you, but oh well. How are you with Excel spreadsheets?'

'I'm okay,' Piper nodded. Excel wasn't exactly her favourite program, but she'd used it plenty of times.

'Wonderful. Can you please meet Mason in the boardroom at four o'clock?' she asked. 'He needs some help.'

8

Frigging spreadsheets.

As Piper walked towards the boardroom she thought about what life would have been like if things had gone according to plan. She'd be starting her uni course in exactly a month. She'd be moving to Brisbane and settling into the cute little house that Ally and Sarah had found, and another phase of life would be about to unfold. But here she was, in Melbourne, about to fill in spreadsheets.

Some huge trunks, pushed by a stork-like girl in ridiculous heels, barrelled down the hallway towards her, and she flattened herself against the wall get out of the way.

When Piper finally found the boardroom, she noticed that

instead of the usual glass doors that allowed people to see what was going on inside, the door was a rust-coloured sliding panel.

It was slightly ajar. Piper peered inside. There was Mason, sitting with his back to her. He had his phone in one hand, and the other hand was running through his dark, wavy hair.

Piper knocked at the panel and bit her lip nervously as Mason turned around and waved her in, still on the phone. He was wearing a suit jacket and white-collared shirt with the top two buttons undone.

Piper ran a hand down her pinstriped skirt, smoothing the creases.

'Okay, so we're all sorted, right?' Mason said into the phone. 'Can you get him to clear out his desk tomorrow so you can pass his laptop on to another department?'

Piper winced. Obviously someone else had been axed. She looked down at the granite floor, then back at Mason. He didn't seem to be too troubled about the situation.

Mason finished the call and put his phone on the table. He looked expectantly at Piper.

She was suddenly nervous. Should she introduce herself, even though they'd sort of met already? Before her brain knew what was happening, her mouth launched in.

'Hi, I'm Piper. I met you yesterday, which was when I started. I was the one with the dog in the office. It was Rose's dog, but I guess you know that. Vivian asked me to walk him. I'm working with Vivian. And Lucy, of course.' God, she was babbling. *What is it about this guy that makes me turn into an instant idiot?* She took a deep breath and made herself slow down. 'Rose asked me to come and help you.'

'Great,' said Mason, smiling. Despite the fact that she'd been rambling like a maniac, he looked at her as though she was exactly the person he needed for this job. He got up and slid the door shut behind them.

Piper had expected the boardroom to have a corporate feel, but it was much cooler than that — more like an amazing warehouse. At one end of the huge room were three thin rectangular windows, almost like picture frames presenting chosen snippets of the outside world. Subtle rectangular rays of light fell across the table of blond wood in the centre of the room. The chairs around the table were covered in soft ponyskin, the tan-and-cream patterns a little different on each. A large screen on one wall featured the image Piper had seen yesterday on Rose's desk: the angular model in gold chiffon, rising out of a waterfall.

'All right, Piper,' said Mason, 'here's the gig.' He switched on some lights above the boardroom table, then pulled out a chair and motioned for Piper to sit down. She was glad — her legs had weirdly started to feel like jelly.

She waited while Mason set things up. He lay some A3 printouts on the table in front of her. Then he opened his laptop, and leant across to click open an Excel file. As the spreadsheet opened up, Piper became distinctly aware of how close Mason was. She noticed the line of his jaw. *Chiselled,* she was sure it would be called. She was close enough to see the pulse in his neck, moving the skin a tiny fraction, in and out.

Piper tried to focus on the spreadsheet. It looked complicated. There were loads of worksheets in the file, full of colour-coded figures with formulas attached.

'It's bit of a dry task, but an important one,' Mason explained. 'I'll need you to work on a master spreadsheet, so we can combine all the figures in these worksheets.' Piper could smell a combination of things: his soap, his deodorant, his skin. 'But we need to add ten per cent to each of the red figures, subtract fifteen per cent from the blue, and multiply the black ones by three,' he went on. 'These are projected outcomes that need to be adjusted according to various market influences.' He looked at Piper. 'Does that make sense?'

'Um. I think so,' said Piper. 'I'm supposed to add ten per cent to the . . .' She could feel his eyes on her now. A little current of electricity flashed between them. 'Er . . . to the red,' Piper felt her cheeks flush. She felt like she'd hardly caught anything he'd said. God, he was going to think she was a complete moron.

Mason went over everything again, his voice calm and relaxed. Piper tried to concentrate and convince herself that she'd imagined that little spark.

'I'm just going to sit on the other side of the table,' he said. 'So if you have any questions, just ask, okay?'

⌒

After Mason had explained the task to her a second time, Piper realised it wasn't hard. The thing was, there were *so many* figures that needed to be adjusted, and it wasn't even remotely interesting. Piper had never liked numbers. English and photography had been her things at school.

The hardest thing was trying to ignore Mason. She didn't know what he was working on, but she got the feeling he was struggling. It was in his pauses. Sometimes, when she glanced over, she'd see his fingers hovering above the keyboard for long periods before a few brief moments of action. Then he'd stop again, his forehead creased, and push his hands through his hair. After half an hour of this, his phone rang.

'Rufus,' Mason said. 'Yes, it will all be ready for Thursday, don't worry. We're working on it right now.' Mason sighed as he hung up the phone. He tapped the table. 'How far off are you from finishing, Piper?' he asked, looking over at her.

'Um, a while,' she said apologetically. It was a big job, and there was no point rushing it and making a mistake.

'Do you think you could work back a bit tonight?' he asked, as though he knew it was a favour. 'I really need to firm up those figures.'

'Of course,' Piper found herself saying, and she must have been a bit delirious from the numbers in front of her because then she added, 'YOLO.'

Mason grinned. 'I know, it's riveting stuff. I'll get some food sent in. How do you feel about pizza?'

At the mention of food, Piper realised she'd missed lunch. She was starving.

'I feel great about pizza,' she said. She loved pizza. Especially with strong flavours, like anchovies, chilli, garlic and olives. Unfortunately, it was exactly the kind of pizza that Dylan would never eat, so she always ended up having Hawaiian with him.

'Do you mind if we get one with anchovies?' said Mason, as if he'd read her mind. 'I've got an unhealthy obsession with them.'

'That sounds perfect!' agreed Piper. And her stomach leapt with something that wasn't hunger.

⟡

When they had finished their pizza, Piper got up to stretch her legs. She could feel Mason's eyes on her.

'Tell me,' he said slowly. 'What do you think about *Aspire*?'

Piper had started to feel more relaxed with Mason as the evening wore on – she hadn't said or done anything stupid, so that was a definite improvement. But this question caught her off guard.

'Oh, um. It's great,' she said. 'I mean, the people seem nice. Mostly. Rose is great.'

'Yeah,' Mason agreed. 'Rose is great. But I mean, what do you think about the magazine itself?'

'Oh!' said Piper. 'Well. It's very good. It's fine. Especially if you like fashion and dieting and all that.'

Mason looked down at the empty pizza box between them. 'Do *you* like fashion and dieting? Do *you* like the magazine?' he pushed.

Piper crinkled her forehead, unsure of how to respond.

'I just want your opinion,' Mason said encouragingly. 'I trust your good taste. I mean, as an anchovy-with-extra-cheese enthusiast, what do you think about a magazine full of dieting tips?'

Piper laughed. 'You sure you want my opinion? This is, like, my second day here.'

'Exactly!' said Mason. 'You haven't been tarnished by the industry yet. I'm interested to hear what you think. Tell me. Would you buy the magazine for yourself?'

'Um. No. Well. It's not my kind of magazine, if I'm being honest,' Piper said carefully.

Mason didn't seem upset. Or surprised. 'So, would you buy the magazine if it were different, somehow?'

'Sure,' said Piper. 'I like that glamorous high-end fashion feel it has. But, well . . . '

Mason nodded, encouraging her to go on.

'I think the articles need to be better,' she began, thinking of Wendy and her desire to deepen the article she was working on. 'There are enough magazines out there making women feel like shit. The magazine is called *Aspire*. What do women aspire to? It shouldn't be just looking good. I'm sure they aspire to have interesting conversations, and to know more – not just read celebrity gossip.' Piper warmed to the topic. 'It's possible to do more. One of the best articles I've read in a magazine lately was a series of interviews in *Marie Claire*. I can't remember what it was called, but it was about four twenty-year-old women from all over the globe, exploring their views on sex and love and marriage. Instead of something like that, *Aspire* seems to prefer to focus on snippets and grabs that never really go anywhere. And,' Piper said, getting to her main problem, 'I hate the way so many magazines make you feel bad about yourself. There's always that implication that the reader isn't quite sexy enough, or skinny enough, or rich enough. If I'm going to buy a mag, I want to feel better about myself after reading it, not worse!'

'I see,' said Mason.

Piper was on a roll now. It was great to give a release to the thoughts that had flown through her mind when Wendy was in Rose's office. And more opinions kept coming to her as she spoke. She was so in the moment that she didn't even think of how she might sound or look while talking, or how Mason was receiving her views.

'The fashion is great. It's ridiculously expensive, of course. So no-one I know could actually buy it. But that's okay – it's kind of arty. But to me, it just seems silly to have such frothy articles alongside it. They're so shallow, it almost makes the clothes look bad. It's like the magazine is for people who are either rich enough to buy the clothes or dumb enough to read the articles. Or both rich and dumb. And that's not a great market. You know? Where's the stuff for people who have half a brain?'

For a while Mason didn't say anything, and Piper was sure she'd gone too far.

'I'm sorry,' she said quietly. 'That was kind of a rant.'

'No,' said Mason slowly. 'You've given me a lot to think about.' He looked at his phone. 'Thanks for your work, Piper. It's getting late. It's probably time you went home.'

'Oh,' Piper said. She had definitely stuffed up.

She packed up her things. Mason slid the panel door open. The hallway outside was pitch black.

'I'll walk you to the lift. Sorry, the lights turn off automatically after eight, and the manual switch is down near the lift.'

Piper walked down the dark hallway towards the elevator. Mason's hand touched her back lightly, just to guide her. It sent a bolt of electricity through her.

'You know . . . ' Mason's voice was smooth in the darkness. 'You're really not afraid to speak your mind.'

Piper thought she heard him add, 'I like that.' But it was spoken so softly, she began to doubt if he'd said anything at all.

For a moment, they stood in front of the elevator doors. Piper stared at the two square buttons, lit around the edges, pointing in opposite directions. One up, one down. She could hear Mason breathing next to her. His smell — aftershave, soap, whatever it was — was divine. His hand was still lightly on her back. In the darkness, it was almost possible to forget who he was. He was a shadow, sending electricity along her spine with his slightest touch, and she wanted his hands all over her.

'So, thank you,' Mason said suddenly. 'And, er, thanks for staying back.'

He quickly switched on the lights. Piper blinked her eyes to adjust to the brightness.

Mason pressed the down button and the doors swiftly opened with a soft chime.

'The foyer lights should still be on,' he said, and handed her a Cabcharge from his wallet. 'Use this to get home. 'Night, Piper. Thanks again,' he smiled.

''Night,' said Piper, and the elevator doors slid closed.

9

Mason let the Aston Martin Virage idle in front of his dad's bayside mansion.

God, what had he been thinking? He had let his guard down with Piper. He should have handled that situation better.

She was cute and funny. And now that she'd pointed it out, he could see what she'd said about the magazine was entirely true. He hoped his jaw hadn't dropped when she mentioned the great article she'd read. A fellow passenger had handed a mag to him on the long plane trip home from the States. Despite not normally being remotely interested in women's magazines, he had read every amazing word in very article Piper had mentioned. The writer was so good that she made a twenty-five-year-old Anglo-Saxon male feel what it might be like to be a twenty-year-old Pakistani woman. He had googled the writer when he got home. Megan Roach, a freelance journalist, had won the Best Article of the Year three times running at the Australian Publishers Excellence Awards.

So Piper definitely had instinct in that area. She'd been there for almost no time, and yet she was already aligned with Rose's opinion about the direction *Aspire* needed to go in. An opinion that was starting to gel with Mason, despite the risks involved.

He almost wished that Piper hadn't said any of it — because it made him see that she wasn't just cute and funny, but intelligent and switched on too.

Why did he have to go and order pizza, like they were on some kind of teenage date?

The way she devoured that pizza was a complete turn-on. The way she laughed without pretension. In the dark hallway he would have liked to slip his arms around her waist. He'd flicked on the lights as soon as he could, just to stop himself from having those thoughts. She was an employee! Jesus.

Mason shook his head. He really needed to refocus. To get her out of his head and solve the various crises that threatened to swamp him completely. And then get out, back to the States, where he needed to start his real career.

Mason hit the steering wheel with the palms of both hands. He stared through the windscreen and out across the choppy water in the darkness.

His phone rang. *Kara*. He took a deep breath and pulled himself together. She needed him. And, to be honest, he needed her too.

'Mase,' Kara said when he picked up, 'too much bloody phone tag. Did you get my voicemails on Wednesday?' She sounded okay. Better – clearer than she'd sounded for a while, actually.

'Yeah,' Mason replied. 'Sorry. I was flat out that day.'

Kara didn't contest this, but it was obvious she knew what was going on. Mason *always* took Kara's calls, regardless of what he was doing. But last Wednesday, he took only work calls. He'd been so busy, there was no time for emotions. *This* year, on the anniversary of his mum's death, he couldn't even share memories of her with his father.

'I lit a candle for her,' Kara said. 'Well, several candles actually.'

Mason had a sudden flash of his mum before she got sick. Of himself as a little boy, feeling so grown up at being allowed to strike a match and light a candle by himself. Then the memory drifted back to wherever it came from. He opened his eyes.

'Mase. Are you okay?'

'Yeah, of course,' he said. 'I've just got a lot on, with work and Dad and all.'

He could hear Kara filling up a glass. 'Christ, and I'm not helping, am I? Making you play my crazy game. That stupid tabloid dropping you in it. You must be so sick of it all.'

Even though Kara couldn't see him, Mason shook his head. They'd been through this all before. 'Kazzy, honestly, I don't mind.'

He could picture her reaction. The nickname that had followed her through their teenage years. Even then, she'd hated being called Kazzy. He used to do it to tease her. Well, actually, it was probably more about provoking her. If their first physical contact was her punching him, he'd be up for it. It was a teenage flirting strategy of sorts, with plenty of room for development. Well, that's what he'd thought at the time.

'If you call me that again, I'll have to drive over there right now to thump you,' she said, rising to the bait as always.

'All right. I'll consider myself warned,' he said, considering whether he might risk one tiny *Kazzy* at the end, just for fun.

But Kara started talking again. 'Honestly Mase,' she said, 'I just don't want to do this to you anymore. I feel like I'm stuck between a rock and a hard bitch.'

Mason smiled. 'You could always give Anita a few tips on what to do with her *advice*,' he said. 'I've got a few creative suggestions if you're short on ideas. But it has to be your decision, Kara. And there's no rush. Not from my end anyway. You've got a full schedule for the next few weeks. Maybe you should take some time off to think about it properly after the supermodel shoot?'

Mason could hear Kara munching at the other end of the phone. It would be Twisties for sure. They'd been Kara's thinking food since Mason first knew her. Since he fell in love with her when they were teenagers. Rose had introduced them when Kara was doing her first shoot – Kara had been from out of town, with no friends in Melbourne; Mason had been more than happy to oblige. The two of them had kind of grown up together from then on.

Right from the beginning, they cared for each other. Mason had Kara — as well as Rose and his father — to thank for stopping him from completely spinning out of control after losing his mum. He'd cared for Kara, too, when she was all alone in a new city. It felt like love.

And it was love, just not the kind that Mason had in mind. That side of things had been a struggle. In fact, lots of the stuff between Kara and Mason had been a struggle. A bit of a train wreck, really. But what they'd salvaged was precious.

'Are they chicken or cheese Twisties?' he asked.

'A combo,' Kara replied. 'Desperate times.'

'Better go for a run around the block afterwards,' Mason joked. As both of them knew, Kara's stress levels were a great calorie burner.

'Seriously though, Mase, if someone comes into your life, someone you want to date, you have to tell me, okay?'

It was absurd that an image of Piper came to mind. Kara was probably doing him a giant favour, taking him off the market. Mason shook his head. 'Kara, I shall die alone, thinking of you.'

'I reckon you should get a few cats,' Kara replied. 'You know, to feed on your decomposing body until the postman finds you.'

'Excellent suggestion. Thanks.'

'No problem. Are you coming to the Bojangles bikini shoot on Friday?'

'I might find a moment to pop in,' Mason replied. 'Apparently my supermodel girlfriend is going to be there. Since she doesn't put out, the least she can do is give me an eyeful.'

'Poor Mase,' Kara said. 'You're the best boyfriend a girl doesn't have.'

'Ditto.' Mason leant back in the bucket seat, enjoying the sound of Kara's laughter.

'Just one more thing. One itty bitty request?' Kara said.

'My firstborn?' Mason joked. If felt good to have a bit of banter. Life had been so serious lately, he'd barely raised a smile. *Except for a couple of moments in the boardroom today ...*

'On Friday, can you please bring that new girl you've got working for you? Piper Bancroft.' Mason's heart thumped hard as Kara continued, oblivious. 'Kind of straight-looking, you know, serious shoes and a little bit bank-teller. Vivian sent her to give me a hand at the Langham yesterday. There's something about her that makes me feel ... well ... grounded, I guess. And the models I'm working with at the Bojangles shoot are pretty grim. Quite a few *be-arches*, you know. Do you know the girl I'm talking about?'

Mason's eyes rose to the sky. 'Yeah, I think I know who she is,' he said.

'Cool, then. I like her. She's funny. And I think she might actually be *real*.'

'I'll see what I can do,' Mason said, hanging up. He knew exactly what Kara meant. Piper was so refreshingly genuine, funny and cute. But the situation was freaking impossible. She was an employee and, as much as he'd just wanted to have her right there and then in the boardroom, he knew it was incredibly unprofessional for him to make a pass at her.

From tomorrow, I'll make sure it's purely professional, he vowed.

⁓

Mason could tell, by the half-empty bottle of scotch, what his father had been up to that day. Patrick Wakefield lay on the couch in a semi-conscious state, his left hand dangling down, still wrapped around an empty glass on the floor.

Mason flopped into the armchair next to his dad and looked around the giant lounge room. The floor-to-ceiling windows overlooking the beach were about the only thing that felt the same. Abigail had taken things with her in the divorce that had never belonged to her in the first place. In the space where the Brett Whiteley used to hang, only a pale square remained on the wall.

Patrick looked terrible. It hurt Mason to see the sallow skin and slack jaw. He'd been so strong when Mason's mother died. He'd been brave and bold in the face of that incredible challenge.

This man seemed different. Maybe the pain had added up? Maybe Abigail leaving was the final straw?

It didn't really matter. What mattered was getting him better.

'Dad,' Mason gently shook his shoulder.

Patrick edged his way up onto an elbow. 'Mason,' he said. 'You don't have to be here.'

'Let's not talk about that, Dad,' Mason said. 'I'm here now.'

'You're here now,' Patrick agreed, nodding slowly. 'Cleaning up my mess.'

Mason detected moisture glistening in his father's blue eyes. He prayed for a glimpse of the old Patrick, who'd demand a blow-by-blow rundown of everything that was happening at the office if he'd been called away even for a day.

'Do you think she ever loved me?' Patrick asked. Mason's heart sank. 'Do you think she loved me and then stopped loving me? Or did she never love me at all?'

Mason tried to change the subject. 'Rose has come up trumps with this month's cover. I sent it to your email. Have you checked it?'

'I went on the computer today. When I googled Abbie, an image came up of her on his yacht ...'

'Well, anyway, the cover looks great,' continued Mason. 'Oh, and I've fixed the flat battery in the Virage. It's a dream to drive.' Maybe Patrick couldn't talk about work yet, but at least Mason could try to keep the subject away from Abigail. Mason wasn't that into cars, but Patrick had been ecstatic when he'd bought the car a year or so ago. He'd raved about it over the phone, like a child with a new toy.

But when Mason arrived back in Melbourne, the Virage hadn't been driven for months.

'Abbie and I chose that car together,' Patrick sighed. 'She thought it was —'

'Dad!' Mason interrupted. When his father bought the car,

Mason had actually been pleased. He'd wondered if maybe he was wrong about Abigail — maybe she could make his serious dad feel joy again. It was a wonder she hadn't got her claws on the car too.

'What?'

Mason sighed. Obviously Patrick wasn't going to be drawn into a conversation about the business, or even about the car he'd been obsessed with.

'Dad,' Mason said firmly, 'Abigail was a gold digger. She's gone. You need to forget about her and move on.'

Patrick leant down and poured more scotch into his glass. 'Whatever you think, I had something real. At least, it was real to me. Marrying Abigail may have been a risk, but taking risks is part of being alive.' Patrick took a giant swig of his drink. 'Not that you'd know anything about that. It's obvious to everyone that there's no passion between you and Kara. Sorry to say it, Mase, but there just doesn't seem to be any frisson there. And everyone needs some frisson. Better to have loved and lost than never to have loved at all,' he said wistfully. Then he leaned back and closed his eyes.

'Doesn't look like it,' Mason said dryly. He picked up his car keys. He was glad that he'd rented an apartment rather than trying to stay with his dad. It was just too hard, seeing him like this all the time.

Mason drew the blanket up to his dozing father's chin, and switched off the light.

10

Piper was exhausted. It had been a long day, with so many peaks and low points she felt like she'd been on a swing.

She put on her most comfy pyjamas, the flannelette ones that felt like a hug, and sat at the desk in her room. She opened up her laptop and pulled up a blank Word document. What she needed to do was some creative writing. She would start a piece she could use in her next folio. A piece that would hopefully get her into the creative writing course next time.

The blank page was daunting, so she typed whatever came into her head, just to fill the empty white screen.

I will not fall in love with my boss. I will not fall in love with my boss. I will not fall in love with my boss. I will not fall in love with my boss.

She couldn't stop thinking about being in the boardroom with Mason. Seeing the pulse move in his neck. Feeling that flicker of electricity between them. The moment, just before he turned on the lights, when she thought something might happen.

It was ridiculous. In what world would Mason Wakefield, media mogul, A-list nightclubber, boyfriend of a supermodel, be interested in her? And anyway, it was like he couldn't wait to get rid of her after what she'd said about the magazine.

She could hear Dylan's voice in her head. His work philosophy. *Work's work. Just do your job and go home. No big deal.*

Piper deleted the lines on her screen. She closed the laptop and lay back on the pillow, and very soon she was asleep.

In Piper's dream, she was lying naked on her side. A man lay behind her, spooning her. She snuggled back, feeling the closeness of his warm, naked body. He pressed himself against her, and his hand cupped her breast, then moved downwards to where she wanted him. Desire flooded through her as he circled her, and her body responded with a series of small shudders, a pleasant throbbing.

She turned her head, searching for Dylan's kiss. And saw Mason.

Piper awoke, disoriented. That she was in Gaynor's spare room in Melbourne and not her own in Mission Beach was a bit of a surprise.

But the real surprise was the dream she'd just had, and its effect on her body. It was pretty hard to reach orgasm with Dylan in real life – in fact, she'd never quite made it. What was her body doing now, just getting off by itself?

Piper tried not to dwell on it. *Obviously you can't control your dreams – or, it seems, your body while you're sleeping.* Was it a betrayal to *dream* about somebody else? No. Now that she was truly awake, she was convinced it meant nothing.

She picked up her phone and texted Dylan.

Morning, my man x

His reply came back quickly.

Right back at you, beautiful girl.

She stared at the screen, letting her boyfriend's message wipe away any vestige of the dream. She closed her eyes, conjuring up the spooning body, the touch, the feeling of the dream, and put Dylan's face there for the kiss. As it should be.

Then she concentrated on getting ready for work.

She pulled on a knee-length skirt with a frill at the hem and looked at herself in the mirror. She was starting to feel self-conscious about the outfits her mum had helped her choose for work. It was becoming obvious to her that there was nothing there that said 'fashion'. She rifled through her limited wardrobe and pulled out a sheer top. She put on her loveliest, laciest bra, then switched the skirt to a mini she used to wear out partying in Mission Beach. Racy had to be better than frumpy, right?

～

Piper hoped Vivian had loads of work for her. She wanted to be super busy. She needed both body and mind to be fully occupied so that silly thoughts, or fantasies, couldn't seep in.

You probably won't even run into him today, she told herself. *It's not like he's always around.*

She strode quickly into the bustling reception area, setting the pace for the day. Which would have been fine, except that her miniskirt kept riding up. She put her bag on the floor and tugged the skirt down to a better position. When she looked up again, Mason Wakefield was looking right at her. He was leaning back against the reception desk.

Don't think about his cameo in your dream, Piper warned herself. A stupid fear that he might somehow be able to detect how her traitorous body had responded to thoughts of him while she was sleeping rose through her. Every part of her seemed to be on high alert. Maybe it was what she was wearing – there was a lot more of her exposed than usual. But she was painfully conscious even of putting one foot in front of the other, as though the simple task required concentration. To top it all off, she couldn't decide whether to stop and say hello or just walk past.

It was a relief when he waved. Piper felt herself relax a bit.

Of course he had no idea about his guest appearance in her dream. It wasn't like there was a neon sign above her head. What *was* important was that there had been a mutual respect between them in the boardroom, which was great, given that he was the CEO. The rest, the other stuff, was just a distraction she should put out of her head.

Piper decided she'd say hello to him. And she would let him know that she'd remembered who wrote the article she'd told him about. *Megan Roach, Megan Roach,* she repeated inside her head in case she got ditzy again. As she approached the reception desk, Mason moved forward to greet her.

Standing in front of him, it was difficult not to notice how hot he looked in a white shirt and navy V-neck sweater.

'Hi Mason,' she said. 'I remember who wrote that ...'

'Rufus,' Mason said. He extended his hand, reaching past Piper. Her face burnt as she stepped aside — the wave hadn't been for her at all. As Mason shook hands with an important-looking grey-haired elderly man in a suit, he threw Piper a look. He actually looked baffled that she'd even tried to approach him. It was in his furrowed brow, in the way he shook his head. It was a small movement, but it was definitely there.

Awkward. The blonde receptionist, who had seen everything, stifled a laugh and gave Piper a sympathetic look.

He'd made himself clear: she was an employee, nothing more. She'd obviously been imagining any connection between them in the boardroom.

Piper barely knew what she was doing as she walked to her office, she was so lost in a daze of embarrassment. She tried to focus and plan her day. First, she would get straight onto her computer and continue updating the list of stockists for all the clothing labels that were going to appear in that month's *Aspire*. That would mean making loads of phone calls to confirm her information was current. She wouldn't comment if Vivian clicked her fingers or barked orders. She'd ignore all that and just get on with it.

Don't get ahead of yourself, Piper.

Arriving at her office, Piper gave a little sigh of relief that no-one was in there. Even Lucy would have been tough to face at the moment. Obviously the cleaners had been in during the night; they'd moved her Mac and the plug had pulled out from the wall. But they hadn't done a very good job cleaning her desk — there was still a fine layer of dust. She gave the area a quick wipe.

As Piper waited for her computer to start up, she made her first phone call. She was still on hold to speak to the retail manager at Michael Kors when Vivian walked in. She looked as though she'd put on an extra thousand layers of foundation, but it still didn't cover the bags under her eyes.

'What's-her-name called in sick,' she barked. 'Go get everyone's coffee orders, if you're not too special for the job. As in, now!'

Piper walked fast. Vivian without her caffeine fix was not pretty. It certainly wasn't a wonder that poor Bronwyn had called in sick; she wasn't getting paid a cent, and Vivian was such a cow to her. It was a wonder she came in at all.

There was a long queue at Cafe Condor. Piper took an instant dislike to the place — it was jammed with industry types and celebrity wannabes. Piper took her place in the queue and tried not to worry about how long it was taking, but the waiter kept taking orders from people that he recognised — even ones in the queue behind her.

I don't have time for this, she thought, as the waiter continued to ignore her, air-kissing someone else who'd just walked in the door. She turned and walked out, coffee-less.

Surely there are other places around here to get coffee? She cast her eyes down the boulevard. Ice-cream shops, fancy restaurants, designer stores. She veered left, checking the shop signs.

A vertical sign was hanging outside a doorframe. O'Dwyer's. That didn't give away too much. She poked her head in the door. Soft, low music greeted her ears as she stepped inside. Piper relaxed, her panic about getting coffee slipping away.

An older man leant on the bar, a checked tea towel slung over his shoulder. 'Hello, love,' he called. 'Anything I can do for you?'

Piper stepped inside. There were two other men in the bar, drinking something stronger than coffee. Piper guessed the average age in here to be something in the vicinity of *ancient*. But there was something lovely about the barman. His eyes were kind of twinkly, like he was thinking of a private joke.

'I'm just after some coffees,' Piper said. 'Do you . . . um . . . do you do takeaway coffee?'

'Only the best coffee in town,' the old guy said. Piper was doubtful. The place screamed *bar* more than *cafe*. But there was a big old espresso machine at the bar, and she didn't fancy taking a second shot at Cafe Condor, or wandering around looking for another option.

'Okay, here's the list,' Piper said, handing him an order for ten coffees.

'I take it you're on coffee duty. Do you work nearby?' the old guy asked, getting to work at the espresso machine.

Piper perched on a barstool. 'Yes. But it's only my third day,' she said, glad someone was taking an interest in her life, rather than just ignoring her like they had in Cafe Condor.

'New girl, eh? Is the job what you wanted?' he asked, pouring milk into a silver jug.

Piper leant back while he steamed the milk. 'It's okay,' she said. She tried not to look stricken, but the question brought stuff up for her. She was stuck in Plan B. And it felt like shit. God, she'd been such an idiot to even fantasise about getting an article published in *Aspire*. Her job was to do what she was told. Update stockist lists. Run errands. Fill in spreadsheets. Be clicked at. And now she'd told the boss that the editorial content of the magazine was rubbish.

Piper sighed. She'd stuffed up in her final year of school. And now she'd probably stuffed up this job too. 'I wanted to study at university, but I didn't get in.'

'Ah, interesting,' he said. 'You know, I was talking to a young man in here yesterday. He's back in town for family reasons, had to give up his dream job in the States for the time being. I think he feels like his life is on hold while he's here. But life isn't ever really on hold. It just takes some unexpected turns, sometimes.'

Piper thought about this for a moment. 'Like a detour?' she offered.

'Exactly,' he replied. 'And a detour is just a route in another direction, after all.'

Piper smiled. She actually felt a bit better. She watched in silence as the man worked quickly, making all the coffees.

The man placed a couple of takeaway trays on the bar for her. 'All right. Coffee type marked on each lid,' he said. Then he held out his hand. 'Sam,' he said.

'Piper,' she answered, meeting his firm handshake. 'Thanks, Sam,' she said, as she got up to leave. She hoped he could tell the thanks wasn't only for the coffee.

11

The week had gone quickly; it was Friday already. In fact, Piper dared to think as she walked past the art gallery towards the *Aspire* headquarters, it had gone pretty well. Vivian had given her plenty of boring tasks, like checking off stock for upcoming shoots and making sure everything was dry-cleaned and ready to go back to the suppliers. But Piper had done everything she'd been asked to do, and Vivian, too busy to spread her regular cheer through the fashion department, hadn't bitten Piper's head off for a while. When Rose had announced that the month's *Aspire* was ready for press, Piper felt like she'd played a small part.

In a way, Vivian had been right. Piper *had* got ahead of herself with the 'Sheer Sense' article. Obviously, it was nowhere near good enough to publish. She hadn't even looked at it again. The best thing to do was to settle into her *actual* job.

It was nice, too, not having that nervy feeling she'd suffered the first few days she walked into the building. *That* feeling only seemed to happen when Mason Wakefield was around. Thankfully, she hadn't had anything to do with him directly since the awkward moment in reception. Seeing him at a distance was manageable – she'd seen his back in the hallway twice. And through Rose's office windows once. And sitting on Wendy's desk in the features department twice. Not that she was counting.

Piper liked how the receptionists now just looked up and nodded as she walked through the foyer. Angela had even taken to giving her a proper smile. It was as though her time of being the new girl was coming to a close.

Now I can just be myself and get on with it, as she'd told Dylan in one of their nightly phone calls.

In the fashion department, Lucy looked frazzled. She was struggling with a box.

'Last-minute props for the Bojangles shoot,' she said, even before Piper asked a question.

Piper dumped her handbag on her chair and gave Lucy a hand, before starting up her computer.

'Did you know you're coming to the shoot today?' asked Lucy. 'I've got the list here, and you're on it. Assisting Kara.'

This was news to her. 'Okay,' she shrugged. She hoped Kara was in a better state today.

Piper opened her email and instantly felt her heart in her mouth. A message from Mason Wakefield. *Subject: Work attire.*

She opened the message.

Piper, you are required to attend the Bojangles shoot today.

This means you will have to dress like you work for a fashion magazine. While I have enjoyed seeing your transition from bank teller to nightclub dancer this week, I think you could use a small amount of guidance in this area. Albert will be expecting you in the dressing room this morning.

Please meet me in reception at 1 p.m. sharp. I will take you to the shoot where you're to be on hand to assist Kara Kingston.

Mason.

'Oh my god,' Piper gasped. *So much for being myself and getting on with the job.* 'Look at this email.'

Lucy rushed over and read the email over her shoulder. She tapped her tongue stud against her teeth. 'Ooh, burn. Don't take it to heart, Piper, he's just flexing his muscles.'

But Piper felt crushed. Despite seeming interested in her opinion when they'd eaten pizza in the boardroom, it was clear Mason thought she wasn't good enough for the magazine. Her fake Marc Jacobs bag hadn't fooled anyone – except herself. She looked down at today's outfit: the black mini again with a black bandeau and an unbuttoned white shirt over the top. *Nightclub dancer!*

'Piper, you're okay, right?' Lucy's voice interrupted her thoughts. 'There's an upside, you know, so milk it,' she said. 'Albert will have amazing stuff that hasn't even made it into the fashion cupboard yet. You're going to get a free makeover from the best in the business.'

Piper could see her point. Maybe she should take advantage of the situation. It wasn't that she didn't *like* designer clothes, it was just that she couldn't afford them. But she was still annoyed. Okay, she might look a bit under par in this glamorous office. But did Mason Wakefield have to be so rude about it? She angrily typed up a response.

Dear Mason

I'm sorry if my work attire is not fashionable enough for you. Unfortunately I don't have the kind of salary that allows me to dress in haute couture every day. If you would like to rectify that, I'd be happy to accept.

Piper

Then she pressed send.

⌒

Piper opened the dressing room door. It was huge inside. A dozen or so clothes racks were dotted around and there were four dressing tables and mirrors running down one side.

Albert looked pretty wild today, with his white Mohawk and a gold three-piece suit. He strutted towards her.

'Oh, goody!' he said, looking Piper up and down. 'I get to start from scratch!'

Piper shifted uncomfortably. *What's that supposed to mean?*

she wondered. So her clothes were lacking something. And obviously she was no Kara Kingston, but still ...

'Oh dear, girl, I didn't mean it like that,' he said, as though reading her thoughts. 'It's just that I normally get the Amazons in here. It will be lovely to work with a *petite* for a change. I don't believe the lovely Lucy has formally introduced us. I'm Albert.'

'Piper.'

'Spin, petite Piper,' he said, twirling his index finger in the air. Piper turned around full circle.

'I've got just the thing!' Albert announced. He searched through one of the clothes racks and came back with a dress. 'This one was a gift from a happy client. It doesn't have to go back to Sass and Bide.' He handed it to Piper and rushed back to the rack, returning with a gorgeous burnt-orange leather jacket. 'Same deal,' he said, 'except this is J Brand. How do you feel about the combination?

'Oh, I guess I could cope if I *have* to,' Piper joked, running her hand over the black mini that now seemed horribly trashy.

Albert laughed. 'See, that's what's good about us small folk,' he beamed. 'We have to grow big personalities.'

~

'Let your hair down for me, dear,' Albert said. Piper released her hair from the ponytail.

'Oh. My. God. Do you get it cut at the *butcher's*?'

Piper rolled her eyes exaggeratedly into the dressing table mirror. She'd been going to the same hairdresser in Mission Beach for years; Leanne had left Piper's school early and got an apprenticeship. Piper had a sudden memory of the familiar salon. Leanne liked to play Beyoncé on full blast while she worked and would argue with anyone who asked her to turn it down. For some reason, the memory jarred. She pushed it aside.

'Settle down, short stuff,' Piper said. In her silver wedges, Piper now towered over Albert. The yellow Sass and Bide dress clung to her body, the diamond-shaped cutaways revealing her smooth, brown skin. Just a hint of cleavage. Even without make-up or her hair done, Piper knew she looked better than she ever had.

Albert tilted his head to the side. His chubby cheeks scrunched up comically with his smile. 'All right, upstart, sit down and let me go to town on that lovely bone structure. Then I'll summon the troops to salvage your poor mangled locks.'

⁓

Piper sat on the turquoise leather couch in reception, waiting for Mason Wakefield and feeling ... well ... *conspicuous*. Did she look ridiculous? She'd been staring at herself in the mirror for over an hour while the hairdresser worked on her and she'd liked what the hairdresser had done, but still, just fifteen minutes after the makeover, she was in danger of losing the initial boost of confidence that had surged through her.

Plus, there was an odd, high-on-a-swing feeling about unveiling her new look to Mason that made her antsy.

Well, if he doesn't like it, he can just go —

'Piper!' Angela had walked over from the reception desk. 'Oh my god, this is sooo not Best and Less. Stand up!'

Piper smiled. 'Ta-da! What do you think, Angela? Do I look more *Aspire*-ish?'

'I think you look more than *Aspire*-ish,' Angela laughed. 'You look like a goddess! Wow. The hair . . . the make-up . . . the dress!' she enthused.

Piper could see from her expression that Angela was being one hundred per cent genuine. And if there was a little bit too much of a surprised tone in her voice, Piper was totally willing to let it slide.

'Unbelievably gorgeous,' Angela continued, 'but listen, Mason has been caught up on a call. He wants you to go up to his office and then you can exit the back way to the car park from there.' Angela pointed. 'Take the elevator; his office is in the top floor. You sexy thing.'

In the elevator, Piper pressed the top button. She smoothed down the yellow dress and adjusted the jacket. The wedges were a bit higher than she was used to, but at least they didn't push her forward. She *so* didn't need to totter in front of Mason Wakefield. She was feeling pretty high after Angela's reaction to her makeover, but the thought of delivering this new and improved version of herself to Mason Wakefield, as ordered, still rankled.

As she exited the elevator, Piper stopped and steadied herself. She looked around the top floor of the *Aspire* building. To her left, at the end of the hallway, through a floor-to-ceiling window, the Yarra river looked picture perfect. In fact, you'd swear it *was* a picture except for the boats and people moving like miniature versions of themselves.

Piper headed into what had to be the foyer of Mason's office. Straight ahead of her was a glass desk. It was unattended, but there was a buzzer and a notice to press it upon arrival. Piper did so, and then walked over and sat down on the sinky-looking, soft white lounge.

Behind the desk was a wall in what Dylan would have described as 'wanky designer brick'. The door in the wall had a plaque on it that said *Patrick Wakefield*. Obviously Mason was using his father's office. It was weird, the way he was tucked away up there in a turret away from his workers. *Definitely arrogant,* Piper concluded.

A mirror panel ran on one wall. Piper glanced at her reflection and did a double take; her new look would take some getting used to. The hairdresser had chopped into her hair, giving it layers and body, while somehow managing to retain the length. The look was wild and tousled. The make-up woman had given her smoky eyes and burnt-orange lips. Despite still being a bit annoyed, Piper had to agree with Lucy — it had been pretty amazing to get a makeover like that. For the first time in her life, she had a tiny inkling of what it might be like to be a model. She couldn't resist swishing her head around and making a sexy pout in the mirror.

'Come in,' Mason's voice called from his office.

Piper struggled out of the lounge and opened the office door.

He sat at a huge desk, signing some paperwork. Behind him, the scene of the Yarra that she had glimpsed from the hallway became a panorama.

Piper waited for him to lift his head. To see if Mason Wakefield might have just a tiny reaction to her, like in her dream.

But when he did look at her, his face was hard to read. He didn't seem to be reacting to her new look. In fact, if anything, he looked *amused*. Just a slight upturn of his mouth, a slight crinkling around the eyes.

Lucy was right. This man clearly thought he operated outside all of the normal rules of propriety. Above mere mortals like herself.

'Hi, Piper,' he said, with a frustratingly cheeky grin. 'Nice outfit. Very fashionable.'

⁓

The more Piper concentrated on not tottering in her wedges, the more tottery she felt. They strode from the elevator towards a fancy silver convertible parked in a reserved spot. Piper couldn't help doing a small eye-roll behind Mason's back as he pressed the button to unlock it.

Dylan's car was a ute. Serviceable and practical. An *honest* car. Mason's car was ridiculously ostentatious in comparison.

Piper started to move around to the passenger seat, but Mason was there before her.

He opened the door. 'Madam,' he said, as if he were a driver.

'Who says chivalry's dead?' quipped Piper.

She settled in the passenger seat and Mason drove out of the car park, putting on his sunglasses as they burst into the bright sunlight. Piper squinted for a while, then she leant down, fishing around in her giant handbag. It was no good. She'd forgotten her sunglasses.

'Check the glove box,' Mason said, looking in the rear-view mirror as he changed lanes.

In theory, retrieving sunglasses from a glove box was no big deal. So the way Piper's hand shook as she reached out, the way she fumbled with the catch, was frustrating.

It felt strange too, when she finally managed it, putting on exactly the same pair of glasses as her boss. But then, the whole situation was strange. She was driving down the freeway in an outfit that probably cost more than she was paid in a month, catching glimpses of the ocean from an Aston Martin convertible.

'They're a good look for you,' he said. 'I think they warrant another Blue Steel moment.' He jerked his head to the side and pouted, replicating the move she'd done outside his office.

As horrified as she was, the fact that he'd referenced *Zoolander*, one of the funniest movies of all time, was pretty cool. And

Mason's smile — now, *that* was truly mesmerising. Something about that smile made him look younger, too.

'I'm sorry, Piper,' he said. 'I couldn't resist.'

'What the ... how did you –?' Piper choked.

He laughed, a deep, throaty chuckle. 'The mirror in the foyer,' he said. 'It's a two-way.'

Piper sank into her seat. 'I am so humiliated,' she said. 'But just so you know, I do have other moves for different moods. Le Tigre is a personal favorite.'

'Please don't be humiliated,' Mason's smile was broad. His teeth were white and even. 'You know, it's great you're coming on this photo shoot. You might be able to give those models a few pointers.'

'Well, my poses have taken a long time to perfect. I'm not sure these models will have what it takes.' She relaxed a little. It was good to share a joke. 'So, is the car new?' Piper asked.

'It's not mine. It's my father's,' Mason answered.

'Oh, and he's on holidays, right?' Piper said conversationally. 'Where did he go?'

Piper was probably imagining it, but it seemed like Mason's jaw was suddenly clenched. His answer was a long time coming.

'I don't normally discuss his choices. It's personal.'

Piper felt her body stiffen. *God, this guy is difficult.* She wanted to shout, *It's a simple question. I was just making conversation.* Suddenly, Piper felt like they hadn't just shared a joke. More like the joke was on her. She crossed her arms.

114

He was making it clear that she was not on his level. He could laugh at her and order her around, but she didn't have the right to ask even the most basic of questions.

'You know, I don't normally change my appearance on demand,' she snapped, uncrossing her arms and gesturing to the new outfit. 'That's pretty *personal* too.'

'I'm sorry, but we're in a shallow industry, Piper,' Mason shot back. 'Image is important. I make no apologies for that. When you're out and about, you represent *Aspire*. The paparazzi have been tipped off today. They might be filming the shoot. Which means more exposure for us, more for the sponsor. Anyone who gets into the frame, male or female, accidentally or otherwise, has to look the part. There's nothing personal about it.'

Piper felt like she'd been trumped. She should have kept her mouth shut. It was harsh, but of course it was true. Her mum's idea of business clothes was not the same as what you wore to a high-profile fashion shoot. Neither were the black miniskirt combinations she'd been coming up with.

Why did I send that email? Piper wondered, a wave of regret hitting her. *Is he going to sack me?*

She felt so confused — being with Mason was an emotional roller-coaster. He had seemed so friendly when they were eating pizza the other night, and just two minutes ago, they'd been laughing together. But he'd basically ignored her in reception the other morning. Now this. Why was he so hot and cold?

'I . . . um . . . I overstepped the mark with my email,' she said.

'And with what I just said. It won't happen again.'

She hoped her tone was businesslike. She hoped he didn't notice her left hand gripping the leather upholstery nervously.

'Apology accepted,' Mason said.

There was another long, uncomfortable pause. Piper searched her mind for something to fill it. Definitely not *Actually, I didn't freaking apologise*, which was the phrase on the tip of her tongue. She should say something sensible, something totally related to work and nothing else, to get things back on track.

'So, what will I be required to do for Kara today?' she asked.

'I'm sure she'll let you know.' When he turned sideways to look at Piper, his face seemed softer. 'She likes you, Piper. She thinks you're down-to-earth. Maybe we'll have to pay you a bit more.'

This guy is infuriating, thought Piper, as Mason took a sudden turn off the freeway and pulled into a beachfront car park. The car came to a halt out the front of an old weather-beaten timber cafe.

'We have arrived, Madam,' he said, and got out to open the passenger door for her.

12

Piper was glad Mason had been whisked away by two photographers just seconds after he'd opened the car door for her. Being around him was unsettling. Now, in the car park, she felt like she was returning to her senses for the first time since leaving the *Aspire* offices. There were so many vans and cars parked there, it was a bustle of activity. In one corner of the car park she spotted Larry, Kara's bodyguard, leaning against a gleaming limousine. Nearby, there were men unpacking cameras and lighting equipment. A woman with a seventies-style afro struggled to push a clothes rack up a ramp to the cafe. Piper could only see the shapely legs of another woman as she lugged loads of colourful caftans over her shoulder.

Once inside the cafe, Piper realised the shoot was actually organised chaos. People scurried in every direction, talking on mobile phones and giving directions. A tall, skinny man in a colourful sarong and a cropped grey fur coat had bailed up Mason, and the two photographers in the centre of the room, and was gesturing madly as he spoke. The sarong and coat combination seemed an odd choice to Piper but, as she had been bluntly informed, she wasn't equipped to judge fashion choices. Perhaps it was a case of knowing what the rules were before you could break them. Piper figured he must be Mr Bojangles, the swimwear designer. Next to him, Mason looked conservative in both his looks and his manner. As much as Piper didn't like to admit it, even to herself, he looked grounded and calm in contrast. Like everything was under control now that he had arrived.

Piper pulled her eyes away and scanned the room. Cafe tables and chairs were stacked high in one corner. In front of them, loads of tables had been pushed together and stacked with beauty products. A make-up artist was applying foundation to an incredibly pretty boy's chiselled features. Another had just applied false eyelashes to a bikini-clad model and was standing back to check they were attached properly, while the girl blinked. Two hairdressers worked side by side: one used a flat iron on one model, and the other used curling tongs on another.

In one corner, a few sheets had been slung haphazardly, shielding only parts of an array of ridiculously perfect, half-naked female bodies in various stages of undress. Another gap showcased glimpses of men's abs and torsos, some slim, some buffed, all completely and utterly toned. Piper did a double take as an impossibly gorgeous naked bum appeared in a gap as though demanding its moment in the spotlight. Piper couldn't help staring, until it was covered with board shorts.

'Checking out the scenery?' It was Lucy, walking towards her. 'Wow, Albert worked his magic,' she said, motioning up and down at Piper's new look. 'You look hot, Piper Bancroft. What did Mason say?'

Piper looked around to check Mason wasn't nearby before she answered. 'Apparently we're *in a shallow industry, so it's necessary to dress appropriately*,' Piper said with a smirk. 'Do I look shallow enough?'

Lucy chuckled. 'Hmm. Maybe get your nose done and come back to me,' she quipped. Even though she was being entertaining, Piper could tell that Lucy was in work mode. She ran a finger over a list she had on a clipboard. Piper could see a stack of male names. Below each name was a list of what each model needed for their shoot, with clothing items and style numbers. 'Last time I saw Kara she was in with the other girls. Just focus on looking after her, Piper. I've got to run. Got to dress the boys.' Lucy looked over her shoulder and winked as she walked towards the male model area. 'It's a tough job, but someone has to do it.'

Piper grinned as she walked towards the girls' section. She spotted Kara Kingston in a silver one-piece, cut away at the waist but held together at the belly with a single silver ring.

The depressed, drunken Kara that Piper had encountered at the Langham was gone. This Kara was in confident-supermodel mode. Her smooth, golden skin glimmered as she ruffled her dark, cropped hair. Next to her, the perfection of the other girls was somehow diminished. Kara was freaking radiant.

Piper felt foolish for even considering that Mason might think twice about her. *This is the type of woman Mason Wakefield dates, the type who would land on his radar. Of course.*

'Piper, over here!' Kara said, with a wave. As though there was any chance in hell Piper might not have seen her. Kara's smile was dazzling; the gap between her front teeth was somehow a serious fashion statement. She glided over to Piper on red stilettos.

'You look amazing!' she said.

'You should talk!' Piper smiled. She loved her designer outfit, but it was no match for Kara Kingston wearing virtually nothing.

'I'm so glad you came,' Kara whispered.

Piper felt her body relax. Even though Kara was impossibly stunning, and towered above her in all her long-legged glory, Piper remembered their time together at the Langham. Despite the fact that Kara looked alert and fabulous, there was still a vulnerability there that made Piper feel protective.

Kara grabbed Piper's arm. 'Did Mase bring you here himself?' she asked. Piper listened for a note of tension at the mention of Mason's name, but could detect none.

Piper nodded. 'I'm on loan,' she said.

'I love your outfit,' Kara enthused.

'Apparently all my other clothes aren't good enough,' Piper said with a shrug. 'I guess I'll have to make this my uniform – there's no chance I could afford another outfit like this. You know, wash it every night, pop it on the next morning and hope nobody notices the repeat.'

'Not on my watch,' Kara grinned. 'I've got masses of clothes. Too many for me to ever wear. Come over to my place and I'll deck you out, girl.'

Piper bit her lip. 'Seriously?' she asked as a rack of clothes was rumbled past, and almost knocked Piper over.

Kara tilted her head to the side. 'Seriously,' she echoed. 'And if you're on loan, I'll have to make sure I return you undamaged.'

Piper grinned. Models of both genders milled all about now. The boys wore very little, and most of the girls were dressed in swimwear and caftans with full hair and make-up. If Piper felt tiny before, she felt almost microscopic now they all had heels on.

'Maybe just some small improvements,' Piper said, risking a few quick points with her index finger. 'A set of those boobs?' she said. 'Or that butt? Or that pair of legs? Honestly, any random combo would do.'

Kara's laugh was more friendly guffaw than a polite tinkle. God, how could someone so good-looking be so nice?

'See, I knew it would help having you here,' Kara said. She put her hands together in prayer position. 'Mase,' she called out. Kara looked up to a mezzanine, where Mason was now looking down on all the action. 'Thanks Mase, you sweetie,' she mouthed, blowing him a kiss. Without a moment's hesitation, Mason smiled at his girlfriend and replied to her kiss with a salute, as though she was the boss.

It was frustratingly endearing.

Whatever the fight that landed them in the tabloids might have been about, neither of them seemed to be holding on to it. Piper brushed the thought aside. It was none of her business.

'So, what do you need me to do?' Piper asked.

Kara ran her fingers through her hair, somehow improving the tousled look. She pulled Piper away from the other models. 'Just hang with me,' she said. 'And bring my dressing gown around with you. These shoots can get a bit . . . well, they can get *icy*.' She lowered her voice. 'It's hard to explain. It's just . . . well . . . things can get a bit hostile and catty at shoots like this. Sometimes I get the feeling that I'm being stabbed in the back, though I could be imagining it all. I get a bit paranoid. I thought it would be calming to have you here. To get your take on things. You know, the opinion of someone real.'

'Okay,' Piper said, though she really didn't get what Kara was asking her to do. Be her hired bestie? Sometimes, she really didn't understand this job at all.

~

An hour later, Piper understood: She was a lackey, but Kara needed her support because it was a tough gig.

She hugged Kara's pink dressing gown to her. It was so cute that Kara obviously loved it so much, even though it was far from glam.

The beach was wild and woolly, all jagged rocks and crashing waves. The sky threw different types of light in strands, from bright to muted and back again. Piper knew from photography classes at school that it would be hard to catch the right amount of light for the photos, but also that the different tones could help make the pics awesome. A photographer's assistant, shoeless in the sea, held a white screen behind Kara.

Despite the cold temperatures, Kara had been posing on her knees at the shoreline for ages. She was very professional. Piper could only imagine how freezing the water that splashed over her might have been. Finally, the photographer was ready to move on to another shot.

A male model walked into the frame. He was naked from the waist up and a little bit too beefed up for Piper's taste. But when he sat on the shore, and Kara lay with her head on his lap, the tender look on his face made him more likable. A lock of blonde hair fell over one eye as he gazed down at her. The photographer walked all around them, snapping away.

Piper felt a frown form on her face. It was weird. As well as looking incredibly striking together, they looked totally, convincingly in love. This was highly unlikely, since Kara had told her she'd never worked with any of these male models. Piper's eyes were glued to the pair as Kara lifted her lips to meet his. The smouldering, lusty gaze she directed at him made her look hotter than ever. *No cheesy Blue Steel for Kara Kingston*, Piper thought. It was probably part of the reason Kara was so successful.

'Jesus, how looooong are they taking? Like, hello, we're *waiting*.' To Piper's right, three models were talking as they waited for their shoot. Two of them, who called themselves Petal and Xena, were uber thin and angular, and had dark hair that cascaded over their shoulders. They wore matching Aztec-print swimwear, one in a bikini and the other in a one-piece. Piper recognised the third model as the one she'd seen batting her false eyelashes for the make-up artist. She had introduced herself as Georgie, and she wore a different, but equally gorgeous, red gingham bikini. She was blonde, with big boobs and a tiny waist. Piper stood apart from them, but could clearly hear their conversation.

'Do you think Kara Kingston is skinnier than me?' Xena said. 'Particularly in the waist. Look at my waist and then at hers.'

'I think you're about the same,' Petal responded. 'But I totally think your legs are longer. It's just that she's had sooo much practice with lingerie because of being a Victoria's Secret Angel, and that's practically the same thing as swimwear, so she's cut all the angles.'

'Actually, you're skinner than usual,' Xena chimed in, her eyes narrowing in an accusatory way. 'Petal, did you do the whole Adriana Lima thing to prepare for this?'

'What's the Adriana Lima thing?' asked Georgie.

Xena laughed. 'Been under a rock much?' She shook her head

in disbelief at Georgie's naivety.

Piper, who shared that particular brand of naivety, moved a little closer so she wouldn't miss anything.

'A month and a half before a Victoria's Secret show, Adriana works out twice a day. She only eats lean protein, green vegetables and protein shakes. Plus, she drinks four and a half litres of water per day,' said Xena.

'Then,' Petal said, taking over the explanation, 'nine days before the parade, she quits eating altogether, and just has the shakes.' She sounded completely reverential, as though she was telling a very serious tale of life or death.

'Twelve hours before she goes down that runway,' Xena continued, 'she stops drinking. Even water is a no no.'

'Wow,' Georgie breathed, 'that's *really* . . .'

'Inspirational,' Petal finished for her. 'I did do some Adriana,' she said, turning to Xena, 'but the no water thing broke me.'

Piper blew out a breath. She didn't share the opinion that starving yourself was an admirable thing, and it looked to her like Georgie was with her. She was about to move away when Xena resumed her examination of Kara Kingston. This time, it wasn't only her body that was under inspection.

'KK might not be as skinny as Adriana, but she still has it all,' Xena said with a pout. 'She's an Angel *and* she's dating Mason Wakefield.' She pointed towards the pier where Mason was watching the shoot with a few others. 'Check him out, he's *gorgeous*.'

As she looked over to the pier, Piper's stomach lurched. Having been ready to shift away just a moment ago, Piper now found that she was rooted to the spot. Moving just didn't seem possible. Not while someone was talking about Mason Wakefield, even if it *was* the Aztec bimbos.

'You know, most guys wouldn't be so cruisy about their girlfriend doing *that*,' Petal said. 'They'd be too jealous. At least, they wouldn't want to *watch* it.' On the shoreline now, the beefy model carried Kara into the sea as though stepping over the threshold with his bride.

Piper imagined how Dylan would react to seeing her in a photo shoot like that. Not that it would ever happen, but, if it did, she doubted that Dyl would stick around to observe.

'Actually,' Xena said, no doubt ready to share another deep insight, 'I've heard loads of people say their relationship is a scam. Like, she was *supposedly* still going out with him while he was away at Harvard? *Apparently*, they didn't even see each other for two whole years. As if either of them could stay faithful for that long.'

'Ooh, seriously?' said Petal. 'God, if it's true, that means Mason Wakefield might be *available*. Stand aside, ladies.' She looked over to where Kara was now finishing up. 'I reckon I could follow that up. She's not all that when you see her in person. There's just something a bit off about her proportions, if you ask me.'

'Well, I haven't heard that rumour, and I actually follow what's going on with them,' said Georgie. 'And I think Kara Kingston is stunning. She's my absolute hero. I met her earlier and got her autograph and she was lovely to me.'

The other two stared at her scathingly.

'Um . . . that's what I think, anyway,' she finished. Piper could see Georgie's relief when one of the photographers walked up to her.

'Georgie, you're up now,' he said.

'Thanks,' she said, with a nod. She turned back to the others. 'Okay, bye, girls. Good luck with your shoot.'

As soon as Georgie got out of earshot, Piper could practically see them itching to bitch about her.

'She's quite pretty,' said Xena, 'if you like those kind of flat noses.'

Piper would have liked to create two flat noses with her fist. Not that she'd ever actually do it, but it was satisfying at least to *imagine* doing it. Those girls were toxic.

⁓

The sun had started to set by the time the shoot ended. Mr Bojangles had made a big show of presenting caftans to each of the participating models. He didn't seem to notice that all of them were freezing, and much more desperate to finish up and get warm than to line up and receive his gift.

'Can I get you a coffee, Kara?' Piper asked when it was over. She wrapped Kara in her fluffy dressing gown. Most people were getting ready to leave after the long day.

'Mmm, yes, an espresso, please,' Kara said between chattering teeth. She gave Piper one of her famous grins.

When Piper returned with the coffee, Xena, Petal and Georgie were gathered around Kara.

'Oh my God, Kara, you were *amazing* out there.' It was Xena gushing. She and Petal were barely covered up. Their red silk robes couldn't have been warm, but they did give the photographers a bonus eyeful as they packed their equipment. Piper could tell Xena and Petal were enjoying the effect they were having on the photographer's assistant. The poor guy bumped into the door and had to re-route.

'I always say to my sister, Petal,' Xena continued. 'I say, you watch Kara Kingston and see how she does it.'

Piper watched as Petal nodded eagerly.

'Yes, that's what Xena tells me,' she agreed, motioning to her sister. 'Because we both admire you so much, Kara.'

Piper restrained an eye roll. *Petal and Xena.* Their names sounded as fake as the compliments coming from their constantly pouting lips. Piper leant over Georgie's shoulder and handed Kara her espresso.

'Oh, I'll have a decaf latte,' Petal said with a flick of her hand, barely even glancing at Piper.

'A soy flat white for me. Extra hot,' Xena added.

'Actually, girls,' Kara said, 'that's not Piper's job. She's my PA today.'

Petal and Xena did a double take, checking out the room as if searching for their own PAs. When they looked back at Kara, their smiles were still stuck on.

'Oh sure, I'll go get *our* PAs to fetch us some coffee. We *so* hope to work with you again, Kara,' Xena said, completely ignoring Georgie and Piper. She opened her robe even more and walked away with Petal in tow.

'You want to know something funny?' Georgie said, moving into the gap that Petal had left. 'I saw their folios because we're with the same agency. Their names are Jane and Jenny.' She screwed up her button nose. 'Jane and Jenny Smythe, actually.'

Piper bit her lip to stop from smiling. 'Maybe they have two names?' she suggested. 'Why not? They're definitely two-faced.'

'Ah,' Kara said. 'I thought I was just being paranoid, but when we were getting changed, those two seemed to be really *assessing* me. They actually gave me a shiver up and down my spine.'

'Well, that would be your instincts working,' Piper said.

Georgie leant in towards Piper and Kara. 'I've tried to be friends with them. But there always seems to be, I don't know, some kind of sting to them. It's like, what they say on the surface is okay, but somehow it always makes me feel like crap.'

Kara and Piper glanced at each other, exchanging a meaningful look.

'I'd say it might be best to forget about making friends with those girls,' Piper suggested.

Georgie shrugged. 'Yeah, I know it. I just . . . well . . . ' Georgie paused. 'I only just came here from the country and I don't really know anyone yet. I'm living in a share house with other models, and that's okay, but they're all really busy and we hardly ever get to hang out. It's kind of . . . lonely. Don't get me wrong, I know how lucky I am to get to do stuff like this. But my family are all back in Wagga Wagga and I kind of miss them and . . . ' Georgie stopped midsentence. 'I am so sorry,' she said. 'Gosh, here I am just talking away about myself.'

Kara reached out and touched Georgie on the shoulder. 'I was the same,' she reassured her. 'How old are you, Georgie?'

'Sixteen,' Georgie replied.

'I was young when I came to Melbourne, too. I was only fourteen. It's not all easy, is it?'

Georgie's lip started to quiver. 'It is hard sometimes,' she said. 'Just trying to be everything the agency wants me to be.' Georgie sighed, but Piper could tell she was getting some relief from sharing her story.

'My agent, Dominic, is trying to teach me how to walk better, you know, catwalk style,' she said softly. 'He's also getting me to work on my speaking voice, because he reckons my elocution is pretty bad and I need to work on that in case I get any speaking parts in ads or whatever. Which is fine. Except that sometimes I just feel a bit like he's trying to fix *everything* about me, like everything about me *needs* fixing, if you know what I mean.'

Kara threw her hands in the air. 'Tell me about it,' she said. 'I've been at this job for eight years and my agent is onto me for just about everything. She's really harsh. But the thing is, she gets results. Dominic has that kind of reputation, too. You just have to tough it out, Georgie.'

As Georgie took in Kara's words, Piper thought about her introduction to Kara's agent, Anita. The result was an involuntary shiver down her back. *Harsh* was an understatement when it came to Anita. In fact, if Piper lined Anita and Vivian up for a catfight, she wasn't sure who would win.

'What about you?' Georgie said to Piper. 'Who's your agent?'

Piper choked back a giggle. Georgie and Kara *towered* over her. She felt more like a hobbit than a model in their company.

'I'm not a model,' she said, 'though big thanks for asking. But I can relate. My boss is pretty full on. With Vivian, you have to hang onto your self-esteem with an iron grip or it'll be gone for good. She does this a lot.' Piper clicked her fingers in Georgie's face to demonstrate Vivian's attitude. 'You. Coffee. Now. And don't get *ahead of yourself*.'

Georgie gasped. 'That's pretty wrong.'

'See, we're all survivors,' Kara said with a smirk. 'We should go on one of those reality shows where you have to put your hand in a fish tank full of scorpions.'

'Too easy,' Piper joked back, 'compared to hearing whatever comes out of Vivian's collagened lips.'

'I've met Vivian,' Kara said, 'and her collagened lips are sweetness and light compared to Anita's frozen face. What does Dominic look like, Georgie?

Georgie covered her mouth with her hands. Then she burst out laughing. 'I don't know!' she admitted. 'He had this massive microdermabrasion just before I arrived in Melbourne and he's covered in bandages. All I've seen of him is his mouth.'

It could have partly been the exhaustion from a massive day, but all three girls completely cracked up.

'You know,' Kara said, wiping away tears of laughter, 'I don't think normal people would even find that funny. It's probably got something to do with all of us being simple country folk.' She chuckled again, as she checked her phone. 'Oh. Mason had to go a while back, and he's asked me to get you home, Piper. How about we all go back to my place? We can have our own little shindig.'

13

'Cheers!' Kara said, holding her glass of champagne aloft.

Piper, sitting across from Kara and Georgie in the spacious limosine, followed suit and the three girls clinked their glasses.

'It was a big day,' Kara said, sitting back and sighing, 'but I bet they got some good shots. Alistair — you know, the head photographer — told me you're a natural, Georgie.'

Georgie beamed. 'I can't believe it,' she said. 'If *any* of my photos make it into *Aspire* I will be rapt.'

Piper let her mind drift as Kara and Georgie chatted away. Travelling in the black limousine made her think about the other amazing car she'd travelled in earlier today. With Kara's boyfriend.

'Yeah,' Georgie said, as Piper tuned in again, 'that's what my boyfriend doesn't get. Sean has pre-ordered twenty copies of *Aspire* from the local newsagent and he's going around telling everyone that I'm going to be in it. But, like you said, there's no guarantees. The photographers took a zillion snaps of so many models today and it's impossible to tell which ones will be chosen . . . and I've tried to explain that to him. But Sean's like, *As if they wouldn't use a picture of you, Georgie*. It's really sweet, the way he believes in me . . .' Georgie's chatter faded. 'I miss him,' she said softly. 'Is Mason like that, Kara?'

Kara cleared her throat. 'It's complicated,' she said. 'What about you, Piper? Do you have someone special in your life?'

She handballed that one, Piper thought. *Maybe she* is *still pissed with Mason, deep down?*

'Yep,' Piper answered. 'Dylan's a surfer and he's gorgeous and I miss him too. Hopefully he's coming down soon.'

Saying Dylan's name out loud made her mind feel clearer. She was glad he wasn't tricky like Mason Wakefield.

Kara's mobile made a *boing-boing* noise.

'Anita,' she said, pulling back the skin of both cheeks tightly to mime Anita's botoxed face as she answered the call.

Though Piper couldn't make out Anita's actual words, her voice on the other end of the phone was as sharp as her manner.

'The shoot went well,' Kara responded. 'I'm a little tired though, so it's good that I've got the next two days off.'

Kara screwed up her face as Anita spoke again.

'Seriously Anita,' she said softly, 'I just —' But she was cut off. 'Yes, I know she's a great personal trainer. It's just that I had plans . . . Yes, I understand, Anita. I'll be ready at six tomorrow morning.'

'Eeek, that's pretty full on after today,' Georgie said, after Kara had hung up. 'I'm definitely planning a sleep-in.'

'Yeah, I'm knackered and I wasn't even posing,' Piper agreed.

The phone call had sucked the energy from Kara. The colour had drained from her cheeks. She took in a huge breath, as though bracing herself. 'Oh well, I just have to take my own advice: tough it out,' she said.

Just then, the limo turned off the road and into a driveway. Kara fished around in her handbag, and pressed a button on a remote she found in there. The giant, latticed iron gates opened.

The house was a perfect square of pure white tiles and glass. A rectangular pool jutted out, impossibly blue and still, at the side.

'Oh my god,' Georgie giggled. 'So, this is what it's like when you've really *made* it.'

Kara just smiled as she got out of the limousine and ushered Georgie and Piper out. She poked her head into the driver's side window and said goodnight to the driver, then she walked up the steps and opened the front door.

The house was as beautiful and stylish inside as it was on the outside. Piper looked around the lounge room. Everything was black or white. The black leather couch was like something from outer space — Piper guessed at least twenty people could sit on it. The white tiled floor was so clean it glistened. The only colour in the room came from two framed photos on Kara's mantelpiece. Piper gravitated towards them.

'My family,' said Kara as Piper looked at the first photo. 'Mum, Dad and my brother, Russell.'

Piper peered at the picture eagerly, wanting to see what tribe of glamazons Kara came from. They looked, well . . . ordinary. Kara's mum was blonde, round-faced and pale – not at all like her dark, exotic daughter with the pronounced cheekbones. Her dad and brother looked like farmers. They were big burly blokes in plain T-shirts and work pants. It was only in her dad's olive skin that Piper saw any trace of Kara.

'We don't talk much at the moment,' Kara said. 'There's a lot they don't get about my life.'

Piper wasn't sure whether Kara sounded sad or resigned. 'I guess your lifestyle is pretty different to theirs,' she said. 'Modelling can be fast-paced, I suppose, with parties and stuff.'

Georgie exhaled loudly. 'True that. I can't think of a way to tell my family or Sean about all the drugs I've been offered since I've been in Melbourne. Not that I'd ever take any, but I just don't really . . .' she trailed off. 'Modelling is a weird job.'

'I hope you stay true to yourself, Georgie,' Kara said firmly. 'There's a lot of temptation to self-medicate in this industry.' She gave Piper a quick eye-roll, as though referencing their first meeting at the Langham.

Piper checked out the other photo. From the angle of the shot, she could tell that it was a double selfie, of Kara and a friend.

It looked like they were having fun. Both of them were pulling big duckface looks, and her friend was flicking her long, wavy blonde hair back with one hand and holding the fingers of her other hand up in a peace sign. It was the sort of photo Piper had taken with Ally and Sarah zillions of times.

'Hey, was that the girl in . . .' Piper stopped herself. She was sure this girl in the foreground of the tabloid photo that had made Kara so upset at the Langham the other day, but it was stupid to remind Kara of the whole thing.

It was too late, though. Kara had already caught on. 'Yeah, that's Laurie,' Kara said, seeming to brighten at the mention of her friend's name. 'She's a DJ.'

Piper had a little pang of missing her own friends, wondering what they were doing that night. When her phone buzzed in her jacket pocket, she smiled. It was as though Ally had felt the vibe all the way up in Mission Beach.

'Hey Al,' Piper said. 'What's up? What are you doing tonight?' She waved to Kara and Georgie as they moved into the kitchen.

'Ab-so-lutely nothing,' Ally said. 'Unless I want to go to The Shrubbery with Mum and Aunty Lou. Harry's gone fishing with his dad and Sarah has to stay home for her mum's birthday dinner. Another thrilling night in Mission Beach. What about you?'

Piper cupped her hand over her mouth and whispered into the phone. 'I'm at Kara Kingston's house! With her and another model. We've just come back from a shoot for Bojangles swimwear.'

'You. Are. So. Not!' Ally squealed. 'I'm so jealous!'

'And I'm desperate to rub it in,' Piper joked. 'But listen, they're sort of waiting for me, so can I call you tomorrow?'

'Yeah ... okay.' Ally sounded hesitant.

'Or is there something you want to talk about?' Piper asked.

'Oh ... it can wait,' Ally responded.

'Al!' Piper said. 'What is it?'

She heard Ally taking a breath. 'Okay, it's probably nothing. I just thought ... Well, I just wanted to tell you that I saw Dylan's ute out the front of Leanne's house pretty late last night.'

Piper frowned for a second, considering the information. Now she understood why Ally was calling. It was sweet of her – but totally unnecessary. 'Did you see Dylan at all today?' she asked.

'Yeah, I ran into him at the supermarket.'

'And did he have a new haircut?'

'Actually ... yeah,' Ally said.

'Well, there you go,' Piper said. 'Thanks for looking out for me, Al. But Leanne does haircuts from her place sometimes, for a bit of extra cash outside the salon.'

'Oh,' Ally said. 'I didn't think of that. But it's just –'

'Sounds like you've got Mission Beach Malaise,' Piper laughed. 'I know, because I've had the same illness. Symptoms include over-analysing. Solution is to get out of the house. Get thee to The Shrubbery, Al.'

Piper expected Ally to laugh with her. She and Ally always used to play around with quotes from *Hamlet* when they studied it a couple of years ago.

'Yeah, you're probably right,' Ally said reluctantly. 'Talk soon, Piper.'

Piper hung up the phone and walked into the sleek kitchen. There was no-one there.

Kara's voice floated down the stairs. 'We're up here, Piper.'

Kara's bedroom and ensuite took up the whole second storey. The bedroom, all decked out in earthy colours, was much warmer compared to all the glamour and starkness downstairs. The carpet was cream-coloured and the king-sized bed was covered in chunky European pillows and a luxurious-looking gold and burnt-orange doona. Kara had slid open a closet door along one wall to reveal a little bar with a wine fridge built into the wall.

'Seriously, you have a bar in your *bedroom*?' Piper said.

Kara shrugged. 'It's for bubbles,' she said, pouring a glass of Veuve Clicquot and handing it to Piper. 'Just the essentials,' she added, clinking Piper's glass. 'For the viewing.'

'For the viewing of –'

Piper got her answer before she'd finished the sentence. Kara swung open the door to her dressing room. Georgie emerged, looking gorgeous in a white halter-neck dress. It was the perfect dress for her figure.

Piper wolf-whistled. 'That dress rocks.'

'You really think so?' Kara asked. She took a swig of champagne.

'Well, I'm not exactly a fashionista, as you've probably realised by now,' Piper said, 'but *I* really like it.'

Kara refilled her champagne glass. 'I designed it,' she said softly.

'How clever is she?' Georgie enthused, doing a spin so Piper could check out the back.

Piper shook her head. 'Seriously, it's not fair. You already won the gene-pool lottery, now this. Do you have other designs?'

Kara nodded. She led Piper and Georgie down the length of her softly lit and elegantly decorated dressing room, which held an enormous wardrobe that almost put the fashion cupboard at *Aspire* to shame.

'All these,' Kara said, gesturing to one corner, 'are my own designs. Not that I've shown them to anyone yet. They're probably not good enough to let loose in the real world. But I've been doing a design course online.' She tilted her head to the side. 'I'm just trying to think about what happens when the modelling runs out. You know, when I'm too old and too saggy and no-one wants to see me in my knickers anymore.'

'Yeah,' Georgie said, 'I'm planning on doing a beautician's course when I get older.' She smiled cheekily. 'I think I might specialise in microdermabrasion.' All three girls giggled.

'What about you, Piper?' Kara asked between laughs.

'Well, for ages, I wanted to get into a creative writing course. I thought that . . . ' Piper stopped herself. It was strange that she was using the past tense. But maybe creative writing wasn't for her? She hadn't felt a single impulse to do any of it since she'd been in Melbourne. She sank down on the cream velvet *chaise longue* that sat in the middle of the dressing room.

'You probably don't even need a plan, Piper,' Kara said, as though sensing the doubt that had crept into Piper's mind. 'I mean, you're already working at *Aspire*, so that's pretty cool.' She lifted her empty glass and looked at it as though it were a travesty. She walked back towards the wine fridge.

It was good that Kara didn't wait for an answer, because Piper wasn't ready to give one. It seemed that a lot was changing for her and she hadn't caught up with herself.

'When I work on my designs,' Kara said dreamily, coming back with a fresh bottle and topping up their glasses, 'it's like the whole world disappears. I just get so *immersed* in it.'

As soon as she said that, Piper's mind swung back to when she was researching and writing the 'Sheer Sense' article. That was exactly how she'd felt. *Immersed.* More so than she'd ever felt with her creative writing. It was hard to explain, but Piper gave it a shot. 'They've put me in the fashion department at *Aspire*,' she said. 'And it's okay so far. But the one time I've gotten really excited about my work, the one time I felt immersed, was when I researched and wrote an article. It was just a silly piece on how the sheer panels trend might relate to the lipstick effect theory. No-one is ever going to publish it. But it made me wonder how it would feel to work on something bigger – something more important, you know?'

'So maybe journalism?' Kara asked.

Piper shrugged. It was definitely something to consider.

'Maybe you should work up another article and try to get it published in *Aspire*,' Georgie suggested.

'Maybe,' Piper agreed. 'The truth is I have no real ideas at the moment.'

'Something will occur to you,' Kara said confidently. 'Until then, it's all baby steps. Practice. With each of my designs, I learn something new. The next challenge will be to get some people interested in my progress. Let people know that I have another string to my bow.'

Piper watched as Kara put down her champagne glass for the first time since they'd got there and grabbed a bunch of clothes that were hanging in the self-designed section.

'Actually,' she breathed, looking excited. 'Maybe you guys can help me with that.'

～

Outfit number five was the best. Piper ran her hand over the flowing black silk pants. The dusty-pink beaded singlet top was tight but, amazingly, it felt comfortable.

'Wow,' said Georgie. 'These clothes really suit you, Piper. But this one looks like it was *totally* made for you.'

'It actually does,' Kara agreed. 'The pink really brings out your colouring, Piper. So, do we have a deal?'

'Absolutely,' Georgie squealed, lying back on Kara's bed.

Piper shrugged. 'God, Kara. Of course it's a yes. It just seems — too good to be —'

'Piper,' Kara interrupted. 'This is just business. I want you two beautiful women out there in the world, wearing my creations. The pay-off is, when someone asks you who designed them, you let them know it's me. It's all marketing, it's a business deal. Got it? Let's seal it with a drink.'

Before she got a chance to pop another champagne cork, Kara's phone rang. She checked out the caller ID, and her gorgeous face lit up.

'Baby,' Kara cooed. 'I've missed you.' She put her hand over the receiver. 'Excuse me for a couple of minutes,' she whispered to Piper and Georgie, before starting towards the bathroom.

'Ah, that must be Mason,' Georgie said after the door closed.

Piper's tummy did a little flip at the mention of his name. But it didn't matter. If her body was going to keep misbehaving where Mason was concerned, she would just override it with her mind.

'Isn't it cute that she misses him even though they saw each other this afternoon?' Georgie said.

Piper smiled. Although she wouldn't say it to Georgie, she actually thought it was a pretty over-the-top thing to say to someone you'd seen only a few hours before, even if you were madly in love. Maybe it had something to do the booze.

Piper's head was a little cloudy. An image of Mason Wakefield, teasing about her Blue Steel move with his hand on the steering wheel of the Aston Martin, *did* momentarily float into her head before she was able to swat it away.

'You know,' Georgie was saying, ' I heard that a couple of years ago *Cosmopolitan* in the US wanted to include him in a spread for "The Sexiest Bachelors in America" and, even though he was broken up with Kara at the time, he said no. He told them he might be a bachelor right at that moment, but he was never going to put out his candle for Kara. Isn't that romantic?'

Piper shrugged. 'Yeah, it *is* romantic, Georgie,' she agreed.

The bathroom door opened. As Kara walked back towards them, it was clear that something in her phone conversation had shifted. Kara's tone had gone from cooing to pleading.

'You've got to come over. You promised,' she moaned. Kara opened the bar fridge and pulled a bottle of vodka from the freezer — it was as though she'd forgotten that Piper and Georgie were even there. Just like she'd forgotten that she'd said the fridge was just for bubbles. Obviously, Kara kept harder supplies for harder moments.

'Well, later then. Whenever you finish work. And we can still do that picnic tomorrow. We'll just do it for dinner rather than . . .'

Piper winced as Kara took a massive slug of vodka straight from the bottle. It was like she was trying to drown herself.

'Anita doesn't *own* me. I know and I *am* going to do it. You just have to give me some time. I want to see you.'

Kara finally seemed to remember that Georgie and Piper were still there. 'Hang on a second,' she said. Then, into the phone, 'Please, baby. I'll *stop* drinking if you promise you'll come.'

Piper could actually see the level of vodka go down the bottle as Kara necked it. 'We can go,' she whispered. 'Give you some privacy.'

Kara shook her head violently. '*Please* don't go,' she mewed. 'I don't need privacy. *Please*. You can't. Go downstairs and I'll come down in a minute.'

~

When Kara appeared a while later, the vodka bottle was half empty. This time, however piss-fit she thought she was, Kara was staggering.

'Isss all jusss bullshit.' She waved her hands around. 'There's no waay any of it really worgs. Works,' she corrected herself. 'Iss all pressure then the rest is jusss . . . lies. Might as well just self . . .' She flopped down between Piper and Georgie on the leather couch, her shoulders slumped. 'Self medi . . . cate,' she finished.

Piper bit her lip. She wondered whether the bit about lies had any meaning. Part of her wanted to tell Kara that if her relationship with Mason was causing this much pain, she should end it. What could possibly have happened between this afternoon, when things seemed more than fine between them, and now? Obviously he was pissed off about Anita setting Kara's agenda for the next day, but surely that wasn't a big enough deal to lead to this?

'What were you fighting about?' Piper managed to ask.

Kara shook her head then let it flop down to her chest. 'Iss my fault. Iss always my fault.'

Piper doubted that. Surely, whatever work Mason was doing could wait, since Kara was obviously so desperate to see him. There was no doubt Kara had issues with alcohol, and he sure as hell didn't seem to be helping.

Georgie moved closer to Kara on the other side.

'Sometimes it's okay to have a fight,' she said gently. 'Then you get to make up. He obviously loves you, Kara. I was just telling Piper about how he refused to go in *Cosmo* as one of their sexy bachelors because —'

'Yeah, I heard that one,' Kara interrupted. 'Iss crap. Iss nothing to do with me really. Mase hates that shit. Thass why he didn't do it. We're each other's *excuses.*'

Kara reached out either side of her. 'You wanna know a sssecret?' she slurred.

She leant forward. Piper and Georgie leant forward too.

It was obvious that Kara was under too much pressure. But something else niggled away at the back of Piper's mind. A sense that she wasn't getting the full picture of what was going on. A sense that Kara was holding back something that was so toxic that no amount of champagne or spirits could kill it. Maybe it was to do with work; maybe it was to do with Mason. Maybe it was something else altogether. Whatever it was, it was clear that she wasn't coping. Piper had the distinct feeling that Kara was about to unburden herself.

And she did.

All over the stark white tiles.

14

Saturday morning had disappeared by the time Gaynor came into Piper's room with a cup of tea and a toasted sandwich. She fluffed up the pillows so Piper could sit up against them. Piper had been truly lucky to land a place with her godmother; she felt very well taken care of.

'You obviously needed a good sleep,' Gaynor said, sitting down next to Piper's uplifted knees. 'Big week, darling?'

Piper nodded. As soon as she bit into her sandwich, she realised how ravenous she was. When she got back from Kara's in the early hours of the morning, she'd been too shattered to eat. Kara had passed out right after she was sick, so Piper and Georgie had stayed to clean up the vomit and make sure she was okay.

When Kara had finally woken up, she didn't seem to remember the vomiting incident, and neither girl mentioned it. However, Kara had been really apologetic, and before she called the driver to take them home, she'd invited both girls to a VIP night at a club called The Texan the weekend after next. Piper and Georgie would be Kara's guests and everything would be free.

'A very big week,' Piper agreed through a mouthful of sandwich. 'The shoot yesterday took forever.'

'But was it fun?' Gaynor asked.

Piper nodded. 'It was sort of fun-slash-torture,' she said, thinking of all those hours standing on the cold beach. 'Remind me not to become a famous model,' she joked. 'Gyrating in the ocean when it's zero degrees wouldn't be my thing.'

'Don't become a famous model,' Gaynor replied, without missing a beat. 'Should you choose to gyrate, you can do it somewhere warm.'

Piper laughed.

'And where did these come from? They're lovely.' Gaynor said, nodding at a chair in the corner.

Piper looked over to where she'd hung the clothes from Kara. 'Kara Kingston gave them to me. They're her own designs.' She rested her head in her hand. 'She gave them to me and another girl in exchange for telling people who designed them. To get her name out there as a designer.'

'Wow, glamorous clothes, hanging out with modelling royalty, you *are* hobnobbing,' Gaynor teased.

'You may kiss my hand,' Piper said, and laughed as Gaynor gave her outstretched hand a slap. 'So, what did you get up to last night?' she asked.

'Doing battle,' Gaynor said, with a sweep of her hand.

'Uh-oh, another date?' Piper ventured. 'What happened, Gaynes?'

'Well, his name was Andrew, and he seemed very nice,' she began.

There was something oddly compelling about Gaynor's bad-date stories. Already, Piper sensed a very big *but* coming.

'We met at Spuntino's. He had already ordered champagne.'

'Oooh,' Piper said. 'That was a good start.'

'An excellent beginning,' Gaynor agreed. 'Over starters, we talked about old music. The good stuff. Sinatra. Holiday. Franklin. The best of the best.'

'Great,' Piper knew how much Gaynor loved that stuff.

'Over the main course,' Gaynor continued, 'we discussed movies. Out of ten, we had five favourites in common.'

'Awesome,' Piper said. She studied Gaynor's face. It looked like Gaynor was back in that conversation, enjoying it.

'Yes, darling, it was very nice,' Gaynor nodded. 'We were both having a lovely time. We shared a bottle of red wine and Andrew really loosened up. He told me a little about his grown-up children. He asked me about my career. He even admitted he'd seen me in *Who's Afraid of Virginia Woolf* and had been enamoured with my performance.'

'*Enamoured*? Cool!'

Gaynor shrugged. 'Anyway, finally, we ordered dessert.'

'And the conversation turned to ... ' Piper prompted.

'How much we love our country,' Gaynor said. Piper could practically see a shadow pass over Gaynor's face. 'We both extolled the virtues of living in Australia.' Gaynor paused. Piper knew the *but* was coming and tried to prepare herself.

'Then he leant forward.' Gaynor leant forward to demonstrate, her forehead almost touching Piper's. 'He told me how comfortable he felt with me. And that's why he could confide how much he wished that all the Asians and Muslims and whoever else turned up would get out of our great land.'

Piper pulled her head back, disgusted. 'Seriously?'

Gaynor threw her hands up in the air, like she'd just delivered the punchline to a joke. She was a great actress, yes, but Piper saw something she suspected Gaynor didn't want her to see. A small twist to her mouth. Eyes that glistened just a little too much.

'Oh, Gaynes, poor you. Spending the night with a racist weirdo,' Piper consoled. 'But you'll get back on the horse. You always do.'

Gaynor shook her head. 'No, my darling. I'm done with men.' The delivery was matter-of-fact. It hurt Piper to hear her godmother talk like that. It was so unlike her. She always thought the best of people, always kept positive. 'I am going on one more date today for lunch, because I've already committed to it and I won't go back on my word. But there will be no more tales of woe,

Piper. And after this, I won't date anymore. Isaac was my one true love. I was lucky to have him. Now, I have his memory.'

Gaynor smiled, but she looked less vibrant than usual. 'I hand the baton to you,' she said. 'Is Dylan *your* true love? Is he the one who makes your heart sing? You know, even at your age, you shouldn't waste time on Mr Good Enough.'

A surge of annoyance passed through Piper's body as Gaynor walked out of the room without even waiting for an answer. Gaynor was channelling Piper's mum again. Dylan wasn't Mr Good Enough. He was Mr Right. So what if she'd had a few fleeting thoughts about someone else? Thoughts were just thoughts, after all. Stupid things came into people's minds all the time and meant nothing. Dreams, too, were nothing to do with real life. Piper had dreamt about being a mermaid, but she had never woken up with a tail.

It was actions that counted. Only actions.

And Piper was faithful to Dylan. Just like he was to her.

Piper snuggled up on the couch after Gaynor had left for her final disaster date. She felt she deserved a pyjama afternoon after such a full-on week. But she felt a trace of loneliness. It was lovely to have a day all to yourself when you had other options, but right now she didn't. She could have gone shopping, or to a movie, but it would have been by herself.

In a way, hanging out with Kara and Georgie had been hard because it reminded her of what she was missing. She would go to The Texan in a fortnight but until then she probably wouldn't even see either of them.

If she were in Mission Beach right now she would probably be with Ally and Sarah – or she'd be at Dylan's house. They probably would have had a late breakfast of bacon and eggs and then gone back to bed. Piper's face flushed as she thought of the things they'd done in Dylan's creaky bed.

At first, their sex had been awkward. Piper knew from girlfriends that was to be expected, though, since he was her first lover and they were just getting to know each other's bodies. And there was a feeling of closeness afterwards that Piper adored.

Anyway, they were definitely getting better at it. Piper was sure, too, that she was getting closer to climaxing. The last time, she'd felt like she was on the precipice of something amazing. Her breathing had become ragged and her body had found a rhythm with his. If Dylan could have held off just a little longer, she was sure she'd have got there. Piper smiled to herself, remembering his words.

Sorry, babe. You just … man … you just send me off …

She'd loved it when Dylan said that. It made her feel powerful. She'd been so close to coming that time and there would be plenty of opportunities to make it happen again.

Piper's mind strayed back to her dream about Mason. The thing that happened in her sleep – it couldn't have been a real orgasm. Could it? It had felt amazing, but she just didn't realise her body could just, well, *do* that in her sleep.

Her body was clearly hanging out for sex. *And Mason was in my head because of the time we spent in the boardroom that day, that's all*, Piper assured herself.

She wished Dylan were there right now. She wanted to nestle in to him, and to send him off. She *knew*, she just knew, things would be perfect when they finally did see each other again. He had to visit her. Soon. She switched the TV on for company, but put it on mute. Then she phoned Dylan.

'Babe. Hang on, I'm on site. I'll take you into the office.'

Piper could hear drilling in the background. If Dylan was working on a Saturday, that meant double time. Hopefully he'd have the money to visit sooner rather than later.

'Okay, Piper, I'm in the office now,' Dylan said, the background noise dying down. 'How're things down there?'

Piper looked out the window. The sky was grey. 'Cold and overcast,' she said, 'and that's just the weather.'

Dylan chuckled. 'If I was there I'd warm you up.'

Piper smiled. 'I *wish* you were here to do that,' she said. 'Have you booked a flight yet?'

'Nah. Checked it out yesterday to come down next weekend, but it's pretty pricey. Might try again tomorrow, see if it's any cheaper. Otherwise, maybe I'll look at two weeks down the track. You got anything on tonight?' Dylan laughed, like he found his last sentence amusing. 'I mean, anything *planned*.'

'Not much,' Piper admitted. 'I'm just hanging out at Gaynor's. What about you? Do you have anything on?'

'Ah ... just a bonfire down the beach with a few of the crew,' Dylan answered.

Piper stiffened. A 'few crew' at a bonfire on Mission Beach often turned into a lot of crew. Plenty of backpackers passed through there. Some of them very attractive. Some of them gorgeous, in fact.

'Piper, you there?' Dylan asked. 'You okay?'

She breathed in. What could she say? Of course Dylan had to go out to parties without her. She couldn't expect him to put his life on hold, just because she wasn't there. It wasn't like she didn't trust him.

'Sorry, Dylan. It just feels weird. You going out with everyone, and me being here by myself.'

'Aw, babe. If you want, I'll send you some photos from the bonfire. So you feel part of things.'

'Cool,' Piper sighed. The rest of her weekend now felt like it was going to be long and boring rather than snuggly and relaxing.

She looked at the TV screen. It was a news report showing a throng of people marching through the city, protesting for gay marriage rights. A funny sign caught her eye: *Attention Heterosexuals: We demand the right to be miserable too.*

'I did get invited to a party at some swank nightclub with a bunch of models on Saturday the week after next. Free drinks. But if you come down I'll ditch that. Or I'm pretty sure I could get you a ticket.'

'Models, eh?' Dylan said. There was a pause.

On screen, two guys walked hand in hand.

'Ah, seriously, don't cancel,' Dylan said. 'It's good you're making new friends. If I can get a flight, I'm fine to come along. Want me to check? I can check now.'

Piper could hear him breathing as he balanced the phone on his shoulder while using the keyboard.

'Hey, thanks,' she heard him say. There was a bit more talking. It was definitely a girl's voice. Piper couldn't make out exactly what was being said, but she felt a pang. There must have been a new girl at Dylan's work – all the staff she knew there were male. Piper whipped the thought right out of her head. She was determined not to ask Dylan about it.

'You there?' said Dylan, speaking into the phone again, 'I actually think I *can* get a cheap flight that weekend. Hang on.'

Piper watched a couple on TV, marching with their arms around each other's waists. The taller woman wore a mask with Ellen DeGeneres's face, and the other, Portia de Rossi. The one with the Portia mask had long, wavy blonde hair like the real deal.

Piper wondered vaguely why they were wearing masks. She was completely fine with the idea of gay marriage, and couldn't understand why anyone wouldn't be. If these women were gay and proud, wouldn't it be more effective to show their faces?

Then again, Ellen and Portia were sort of figureheads for gay marriage, and the camera was definitely zooming in on them, so maybe the masks were effective in a way?

'Okay,' Dylan said finally. 'So there's a pretty good deal here. What if I fly down on the Friday night and come back Sunday?'

'That would make me very happy,' she said. 'You sure you don't want me to cancel the club thing?'

'Yeah, no worries. I'll tag along with you. I'd be your plus one anytime, baby. I'll email you the details. Gotta go.'

'Thanks Dyl,' Piper said. 'Love you.'

'Love you more.'

Piper hung up the phone, feeling elated. She felt better about just chilling out now. Like the promise of his visit made it fine to spend this weekend being lazy.

The TV news had moved on, but something made Piper press the rewind button. She went back to the first appearance of Ellen and Portia, trying to put her finger on what had struck her about them. The shot showed the full length of their bodies.

She pressed pause.

'Ellen' was wearing a pretty regular outfit. A cute top. Jeans. Piper's eyes scanned downwards to a pair of emerald-green snakeskin boots, with a yellow trim around the top and a cowboy heel.

Kara Kingston's boots.

15

Piper sneaked a rare private moment at her desk on Wednesday morning to google the tabloid picture again. Even days after she'd seen the TV footage and convinced herself it was Kara Kingston in the gay pride march, she still felt obsessed with the whole thing. There was something intensely satisfying about getting the puzzle pieces in place.

Seen last week leaving the Cristobel Club at 2 a.m., Kara broke away from mag mogul Mason Wakefield. Sources say Kara was comforted by a good friend, DJ Laurie Anderson. Neither Kingston nor Wakefield was available today for comment, but Kingston's agent, Anita Barnes, insists it was just a lovers' tiff.

Piper looked closely at the image. The Laurie Anderson in the picture had blonde, wavy hair. The same hair as the girl who'd been protesting disguised as Portia de Rossi to Kara's Ellen. It had to be her. Piper was sure of it.

It all made sense now. The phone call Kara had taken that Friday night was from Laurie, not Mason. Laurie was the one Kara was cooing at. Laurie was the one who was working late, the one Kara missed. It was Laurie she'd been begging to come over. And it was Laurie who refused to visit that night after arguing with Kara about Anita owning her. That stupid tabloid was right about something. It *was* a lovers' tiff. They'd just screwed up which two people in the picture were the lovers!

God, before Kara spilled her guts, she had been going to tell. *That* was the toxic lie that was festering inside her.

Piper stared into space, ignoring the constant din of phones and chatter that ran through the hallways at *Aspire*, thinking the same thing she'd been thinking for a few days now: *What if Mason Wakefield is single?*

The possibility that Kara was *not* Mason Wakefield's girlfriend made Piper's stomach flip over weirdly. Kind of like she was on a roller coaster and excited, but about to puke at the same time.

This is ridiculous! thought Piper. *I shouldn't be feeling like this.*

But she couldn't stop thinking about it. Why would Kara even bother covering up her sexuality? Piper tried to think back to what Kara had said when she was drunk – something about not being able to be herself in the industry? Even in this day and age, Piper supposed there was still some discrimination against gay people that may have forced Kara to stay in the closet. The fact that gay marriage still wasn't legal in Australia was a pretty good case in point.

But why would Mason cover as Kara's boyfriend? Would he do that to protect her from the media? Wasn't his magazine *part* of the media machine?

Piper shook her head. She may have put the puzzle pieces of Kara's story together, but she'd never understand Mason Wakefield.

Piper made herself click out of the screen and tried to focus on her work, ignoring the chattering of Lucy and Siobhan coming from the fashion cupboard. Today, Vivian had left her a list of tasks to do, which was a relief. All she had to do now was to pick up a Prada gown from the dry cleaner's and to go to Prize Pooch to collect a doggie tuxedo Rose had ordered.

But instead of getting going, Piper just stared at the photo of Dylan that she'd pinned to the board next to her desk. It was one she'd taken of him after a surf, when he'd peeled off the top half of his wetsuit. He was smiling at the camera, the sunlight glinting off his blonde hair and tanned shoulders.

'Hey, what are you wearing to the launch tomorrow night?' asked Lucy, cutting into Piper's thoughts as Siobhan left the office.

'Huh?' said Piper vaguely, looking up.

'You're so out of it this week,' said Lucy. 'Is it because you're missing your boyfriend?'

Piper frowned. 'Maybe.'

'The email went out on Monday. There's a party tomorrow night, so Mason can launch the new company direction. If you don't go, he'll probably behead you.' Lucy picked up a pair of scissors from her desk and slid them across her throat for emphasis.

Piper checked her emails and saw the message from reception in her inbox. *Subject: Media Launch.* How had she missed that?

She needed to avoid Mason. Even if he was single, and even if she couldn't stop thinking about him, he was still her boss. And she had Dylan. If she had to speak to Mason tomorrow night, she'd better keep it brief.

～

The chairs and large table had been cleared away in the boardroom, making it big enough for a stand-up party. Minimalist floral arrangements dotted the room on pedestals, and the standing tables throughout the room were adorned with lilies and candles. The huge screen at the end of the room had moving images of models on the runway, alternating with photos and covers from *Aspire* flashing across it. Music pumped through the space, which was already abuzz with staff, models and members of the press clustered around, chatting excitedly.

Waiters that looked like male models, dressed in tight black chinos and white shirts with all the buttons done up, brought food and drinks around on trays. Piper took an espresso martini from one of them and took a sip. The charge from the combination of caffeine and alcohol was almost immediate, and she was glad. Plus she needed something to do with her hands.

Piper scanned the room for Kara, thinking she might attend her 'boyfriend's' big launch, but couldn't see her anywhere, so she busied herself by looking out the windows. She tried not to think about the last time she'd been in this room with Mason.

Boats glided down the Yarra. Piper settled her eyes on a kayak cutting through the water at dusk. The person paddling looked like he was struggling to get anywhere – Piper could totally relate. She felt like she was paddling awkwardly in the boardroom, surrounded by people she hardly knew or hadn't even met. Even though she was dressed in one of Kara's creations, she was still one of the lowest on the *Aspire* ladder.

She wasn't quite as low as Bronwyn, though. Piper winced to see her, dressed in black and white, handing out canapés. She doubted that Bronwyn was getting any real experience from her 'work experience' – she was more like Vivian's slave. Yet, when she approached Piper, she had a huge smile on her face.

Piper raised her eyebrows. 'You look as though you're enjoying this,' she said, taking a mini quiche.

'I hate it,' Bronwyn replied, still grinning. 'But Vivian has finally promised she's going to look at my designs! So I don't care if she never learns my name or if she makes me clean every toilet in the building. I'm *so* excited.'

Piper bit her lip. She wasn't so sure whether Bronwyn should be so excited about showing Vivian anything.

A tinkling of glasses alerted the guests to draw their attention to the opposite end of the room, where Mason was now standing. There was a hush as everyone turned to face him.

'Thank you, everyone, for coming along tonight. As I'm sure you all know, the past few months have been difficult for *Aspire*, but we've made some significant changes to the business that we're confident will improve our profitability, and I thank all of you for your patience while we've been going through the process. Change is always challenging, but it also presents exciting opportunities and, tonight, we're really celebrating a new direction for the magazine.'

Mason Wakefield commanded the room, and he did it perfectly – with gorgeous cheekbones and just the right amount of stubble. His voice was low and deep. His eyes shone as he continued.

'We want our magazine to reach a new readership. One of our newest members of staff, Piper Bancroft, recently pointed something out to me: all the effort we put into the fashion in this magazine is not reflected by our editorial content.' Piper felt her stomach leap at the mention of her name. *He's talking about me.* She felt her face flush bright red as Mason continued.

'Rose and I have been working hard to develop a new editorial strategy for the magazine and we're committed to investing in feature articles that go beyond the surface and break some of the boundaries of traditional content. We want to publish amazing writing, award-winning writing: pieces that could compete for the Australian Publishers Excellence Awards.

'We're also developing strategies to reach younger audiences, and will be focusing on digital developments. We want this to be a magazine that our readers buy not only for the cutting-edge fashion, but for cutting-edge journalism too.'

The screen on the wall flashed up the first cuts of that month's *Aspire*. Then suddenly everyone was clapping. Piper was stunned. It was a buzz. Mason Wakefield had listened to *her*. People were clapping at *her* idea. Piper took another celebratory sip of her martini as Mason's voice broke into the applause.

'I won't take up any more of your time, but well done, everyone, and please enjoy yourselves tonight.'

A voice came from over Piper's shoulder.

'Hello, Petite Piper.' She turned to see a welcome sight. Albert had dyed his Mohawk black since the since the day he'd helped make her over and tonight he was wearing a white suit with gold buttons. 'It looks like you're keeping up the good work, getting big ups from the boss man,' Albert said, his eyebrows raised. 'And what's with this amazing outfit? It's very Red Riding Hood,' he said, turning Piper around so that he could view her from all angles. 'Where *did* you get this?'

Piper looked down at her red dress, which had a loose cowl neck that draped down her back, a bit like a hood.

'Actually,' she said when she'd stopped spinning, 'it's one of Kara Kingston's designs. She's starting a collection.'

'Well, well, well,' Albert said, 'who would have thought! It's divine. You look adorable, young lady. Good enough to eat.'

He opened his mouth wide and made a biting sound.

'Oh please don't, Mr Wolf,' Piper cried.

Albert's laugh was loud and honky. It definitely made Piper feel more relaxed. Piper took the final sip of her espresso martini and grabbed another from a passing tray.

'You should pass on my details to Ms Kingston,' he said. 'I've worked on loads of shoots for David Jones, as well as some of the smaller retailers. I might just know someone who knows someone who might like to check out her gear.'

'Excellent idea, Amazing Albert,' Piper said, clinking glasses with him. God, it felt *good* to be able to do this for Kara. And to be mentioned in Mason's speech. As though she, Piper Bancroft, might actually be just a tiny bit influential.

'That's me, Little Red. Amazing Albert.'

Piper took a sip of the yummy drink and then another, feeling looser with every mouthful.

Albert leant into Piper conspiratorially. 'So, you look like you're up for a big night, Red,' he said, tapping her glass. 'I'm going to head out to a club and try my luck. I need a bit of a fairytale in my life too. Prince meets prince. Happy ending and all that.'

Piper giggled. 'You know, I think it's a little unfair that it's always the princess that has to kiss the frogs. I think it should be the other way around sometimes. Let the prince kiss the frog for a change.'

'Sweetheart, I've kissed more frogs than you've had hot dinners.' Albert retorted. He spoke conspiratorially, out of the side of his mouth. 'To tell you the truth, I don't mind if one *stays* a frog, as long as he's nice on the inside.'

'Oh, Albert,' Piper said. 'You're so sweet ... in a weird, intense kind of way.'

'I know, right?' Albert said, his deep laugh resonating around the room. 'You're very perceptive, Red.'

⌒

Soon, lots of other people were standing with Albert and Piper. It was lovely to be included in Albert's sphere. Piper only had to offer a word here and there because Albert's big personality entertained everyone. She grabbed another martini. She was beginning to enjoy herself. This launch thing wasn't as bad as she'd thought it would be.

The only problem was that it was hard to get to the food. Piper could see the food trays with mini sliders, prawn skewers and nori rolls that were being passed around. But by the time the trays got to her, they always seemed to be empty. Tucked away with Albert and co., she let herself gaze around the room.

Lucy was nearby, standing with a photographer who was resting his hand on her shoulder. Piper might have been wrong, but Lucy seemed to be trying to shift out of the way. Piper watched Mason walk up to Lucy and the guy. He held out his hand and the guy had to take his from Lucy's shoulder to meet the handshake. As soon as he did so, Lucy moved out of the photographer's reach.

Piper noticed Rose walking towards her. She looked beautifully ephemeral in a white flowing dress with batwings. Bruno was under her arm, dressed in the tuxedo Piper had collected the previous afternoon.

'Bruno is looking very dashing tonight,' Piper said as Rose approached. She reached out to give the dog a scratch on the head. 'But he's not just a looker. He's very therapeutic also, you know.'

Rose tilted her head to the side, questioningly.

'Pet therapy?' Piper tried, knowing she was sounding random. 'Um, Bruno helped cheer Kara Kingston up recently,' she tried to explain.

Rose pushed a lock of curls behind her ear, smiling gently. 'Watch out for those martinis, Piper. They have a kick to them.'

As Rose drifted away, Piper caught Lucy's eye. Lucy mimed surprise and walked over. 'Well done, Ms Bancroft, getting into the boss's speech!' Lucy whispered. 'Maybe I have Mason wrong. He *did* just rescue me from a sleazy photographer. And he obviously thinks you're cool.'

Piper raised her glass and smiled. 'I think he's just mist . . . ' Piper tried again. 'Misunderstood,' she managed.

Lucy wandered off and Piper rejoined the group crowding around Albert. As the lights of the city glittered outside, Albert regaled them with a story about his fling with Elton John, when Albert had been his stylist in the eighties.

Piper looked around the room. The crowd was thinning out, actually. Quite a few people had gone. Bronwyn had left, and Lucy was nowhere to be seen.

Vivian picked up her Chanel clutch and flared her nostrils at Piper from across the room before leaving. Piper had to bite down a smile. She could just about imagine fire coming out of Vivian's nose. She felt quite giggly at the thought.

Who cares about Vivian when Mason mentioned me in his speech?

She looked around again. Mason was still there.

He had been working his way around the room, stopping to talk to people on his way and then moving on. And now he was moving in Piper's direction.

Piper stepped away from the group and looked out of the window. Albert's voice was like a good backing track, lyrical and expressive, though she was no longer concentrating on his actual words.

One of the waiters hovered around her. She took another espresso martini from the tray. She felt wonderful. She was fitting in. If she wanted to, she could start a conversation with *anyone* right now. The first thing that came to mind would be the right thing, she was sure of it. But right now, there was one person she definitely wanted to talk to.

Mason was only steps away from her now.

'Piper,' he said.

A little splash of the martini escaped from her glass, as though it had a mind of its own. She quickly wiped it off her hand. 'Mason,' she replied, smiling.

'I wanted to thank you for your suggestions for the magazine,' he said formally. 'I'm impressed with your ideas, Piper, and your taste. Megan Roach is an excellent writer.'

Piper tried to stop herself from grinning. But it was no good. Mason had even bothered to find out more about the article *she'd* recommended. She beamed.

'So, I hear you wanted to do a creative writing course?' he said.

'How did you know *that*?'

'You'd be surprised at what I know,' Mason said cryptically. 'I have my ways.'

Piper took another sip. She loved how the martini was making her brave. And the idea that Mason had been interested enough to find out stuff about her *personally* was strangely exciting.

'How old am I?' she asked suddenly.

'You're eighteen going on nineteen ...' he started.

'Okay. What else do you know?'

'You're from Mission Beach,' Mason continued, 'and you've moved down to Melbourne to work at *Aspire*. You live with your godmother.'

Piper shrugged. 'That's all pretty generic. Pretty basic, if you ask me. Not particularly surprising.' The way she said it was like issuing a challenge. The way she said it was like *flirting*.

'Oh, so you want something more detailed?' he asked, the sides of his mouth twitching. 'Well, you're not so good with revolving doors, but you're excellent with people and small dogs. And you seem to really like those martinis.'

Piper took another sip to demonstrate *exactly* how much she liked the martinis.

'I know a little about you too, Mason,' she said. 'Shall we play true or false?'

The twitch around the corners of his mouth turned into a proper smile.

'You have an MBA from Harvard,' she said.

'True.'

'Your father gave his business to you.'

Mason's expression hardened and he didn't look so amused anymore, which was strange. He was pretty good at stirring her up – giving him a bit back was fun.

'Not quite true,' he said, his voice dropping.

'No, it's just true or false,' Piper said. 'You can't do halves.' She was *really* enjoying herself now. She took one more little sip of the fabulous drink. Then, she lowered her voice to a whisper. 'And you're pretending to go out with Kara Kingstons,' she said. She gulped down on a giggle. What she'd just come out with seemed hilarious – as though there were several Kara Kingstons instead of one. 'But in fact, Kara is not interested in you at all, Mason, because Kara is . . .'

'Piper,' said Mason in a firm voice. She stopped talking.

Only then did Piper notice there were just a few people left in the room. She watched as Mason had a quick word with a cleaner. He picked up two bottles of water from a nearby table.

'We are going for a walk,' he said when he came back. 'Now.'

Mason's silence as they travelled down the elevator was sobering. So was the cool breeze as they stepped out onto the promenade.

There were still loads of people around. People were out for a boat ride on the river. People who had enjoyed a meal together. People were taking a stroll. People who hadn't just completely fucked up.

Mason's stride was fast and Piper struggled to keep up. Part of her thought it might be better to disappear, to get lost in the crowd and go home. But Mason grabbed her hand and pulled her into a deserted laneway.

'Take a seat. And have some water,' he said. He opened a bottle and handed it to her as she sat on the empty milk crate he'd gestured to.

Piper gulped down the water, afraid of what was coming.

'What do you know about Kara?' Mason demanded. 'And how do you know it?'

Piper looked into his eyes, trying to see him properly. Even in the dark, lit dimly by the light from nearby shop windows, it was too much. She had to look away.

'I recognised Kara in a gay pride march on the weekend,' she said softly. 'And I put two and two together.'

'What makes you so sure she wasn't marching as a straight supporter?' His question only confirmed Piper's suspicions.

'She was obviously with her female partner,' Piper said, feeling suddenly very sober. 'Laurie, is it?'

Mason sighed. 'Does anybody else know?'

Piper shook her head.

'The only people who know about Kara and Laurie are her agent and me,' Mason explained. 'And now you, of course. But Piper, nobody else can know. Not for the time being, anyway. It's very important for Kara's career. Do you understand that?'

Piper stood up. She tilted her head upwards so she could look him in the eyes. 'I'm sorry,' she said falteringly.

Mason's gaze pinned her to the spot. He didn't speak. He was obviously waiting for her to continue.

'I wouldn't do anything to hurt Kara or her career,' she said. 'I promise.'

Piper could see Mason relax, just a little. His shoulders dropped. He moved forwards. Piper could see the rise and fall of his chest.

'Kara is a good friend,' he said, his tone muted now. 'And Laurie is a great partner for her. But Kara has worked so hard to get where she is. If she comes out publicly, it has to be her way.'

Piper bit her lip. 'You're very loyal.'

The way Mason looked at her, she felt like she was being seen for the first time. Piper wanted to place her hand over her heart to feel whether it really was skipping beats.

'Pretending to be Kara's boyfriend has been no big sacrifice,' he shrugged. 'It's just a little bit of media here and there.'

'Yes, but you —' Piper stopped herself. She couldn't say the next thing.

'I can't go out with anyone else?'

Piper nodded.

Mason looked down. 'That hasn't really mattered to me,' he said softly, then lifted his eyes up to meet hers. 'Until now.'

Piper's heart pounded. She moved forward, and felt his hands slip around her waist. He leant towards her, and kissed her.

His kiss was soft at first – no more than a flutter. Then, his lips were firm on hers. Piper closed her eyes. His tongue found hers, and the kiss became urgent.

He lifted her against the wall and a moan escaped her. Mason pressed her body into the bricks and she felt him, big and hard against her. She ran her hands over his chest, wanting to rip off his shirt.

Adrenaline coursed through her, making every nerve ending in her body stand to attention.

Piper had never felt anything like this before. She wanted him, right there. Now.

She fumbled with the belt of his trousers, and felt him grow even harder as he groaned. His lips moved down her neck, his hand on her breast. His teeth bit softly into her shoulder. His hands were under her dress, moving up her legs.

'Oh god. I want you, Piper,' he whispered.

A clip-clip of high heels stopped suddenly. Piper froze. She opened her eyes to see Vivian standing at the top of the laneway, her razor-thin frame outlined against the street light.

'Mason,' Piper hissed.

Vivian was looking right at them. She stood there for a minute, registering exactly what she'd seen, then quickly walked away.

'She saw us,' said Mason. 'Fuck.' He started buckling his belt up again.

In that moment, everything changed. Piper felt exhausted, as though all of her senses had been switched on and off and toyed with. It was like her body had been in some kind of electrical storm, complete with charges and power cuts. But mostly she felt shamed, stupid. She felt herself slumping against the wall.

'Come on,' Mason said gently, 'let's get you a cab.'

16

After Mason had put Piper in the taxi, he went home and poured himself a large whisky. He sat staring at it for a while before taking a large swig, hoping to drown out thoughts of Piper. But he couldn't.

He thought about the way she'd looked at the photo shoot. She was so stunning, it blew him away. The yellow dress clinging to her petite frame. The leather jacket hugging her body. But it was her eyes that just about knocked him off his chair. A smattering of make-up, and they'd gone from lovely to smouldering.

There was something so playful, yet intelligent, about her. Something that made him almost forget all his problems.

God, he thought he'd completely buried the way he felt when

they'd worked late together that day. But tonight, there it all was again, in the laneway. And now he'd gone and kissed her. Mauled her, more like it. He'd completely lost his head. And Vivian had seen it all.

But he couldn't think about Piper in that way. The world believed he was with Kara. And he needed to concentrate on getting *Aspire* back on track, not on dating the junior freaking staff.

Things were definitely improving at the magazine. The board meeting had gone well. He'd already streamlined the business — cutting back on double handling, unnecessary expenditure and clearing up those tax issues. Rose was excited to spearhead the new editorial direction.

But costly mistakes were still being made — like the three garments that went missing from the Marc Jacobs shoot, and the priceless Valentino gown currently missing in action. It struck him that it was perhaps more than carelessness. He'd questioned Vivian about it, but her responses were annoyingly evasive, and he had the feeling that she might be protecting her junior fashion stylist.

It was another thing Mason would have to get to the bottom of. Rose had told him recently that she had a feeling things weren't as they were supposed to be in the fashion department. Mason adored Rose, but sometimes he wished she would ditch her *feelings* in favour of something more solid that he could act on. Better yet, if only his dad would come back on board, Mason could go back to the US and escape all of this.

Mason knew he'd been an idiot, flirting with Piper at the party. He knew he should've resisted the urge, but he wanted her to know he'd been thinking about her. He was glad he'd had the chance to publicly acknowledge how much he valued her opinion.

Last week, when he'd taken her to the Bojangles shoot, he'd just about bitten her head off when she'd asked him about his father. He'd felt bad about it. The truth was, Piper Bancroft put his emotions on a seesaw.

He hated how serious his life had become lately. He'd barely been in contact with the part of himself that liked to have fun. Now he had to be the boss but – more than that – he had to be *seen* as being the boss.

What had he been thinking tonight? Piper was drunk, and he'd kissed her, almost taken her right there. Who knew how she'd feel in the morning? She was probably going to sue him for sexual misconduct.

Mason's phone buzzed. His heart leapt, thinking momentarily that it might be Piper, before he realised she didn't even have his number. It was a text from Kara.

Are you still up?

He hoped she wasn't in trouble. He called her. 'Hey, Kara, you okay?'

'Never better. Are *you* okay? You sound weird.'

'I'll be all right. Just another one of those days.'

'How did your presentation thingy go? Sorry I didn't come.'

'Well, it was okay, until the end, when I screwed up.'

'I'm sure you didn't. And do you know what? I think it's great, this idea that *Aspire*'s taking a new editorial direction.'

'Yeah,' said Mason, noncommittally.

'Look, I'm sorry to call you so late, but I need your help with something,' Kara continued. 'I've arranged a meeting tomorrow with Anita. I want to do it — to come out. Tell me you'll come to the meeting and protect me from the wrath of Anita?'

Mason couldn't think straight. 'Hang on. You're coming out?'

'Yes, I have to. Laurie and I have been talking about it.'

'Okay. I'm flying to Perth tomorrow, but not till midday. If the meeting is in the morning, I'll be there. You're sure it's what you want?'

'Yep, it's first thing in the morning. And yes, Mason, I'm sure it's what I want. I feel really good about this. See you tomorrow.'

Mason hung up and poured himself another generous slug of whisky. If Kara came out, it let him off the hook, and would free him up to be with Piper. *But Piper is still my employee, and therefore off limits*, he reminded himself

His phone buzzed. Kara again.

Thanks for helping me face Anita tomorrow! You're my Prince Charming. Well, you would be, if I was straight!

Mason threw back another drink, hoping this one would be strong enough to clear Piper out of his mind.

But it wasn't.

17

Piper woke up with a deep, unquenchable thirst. She checked her phone. It was 4 a.m. She gulped from the water bottle on her dressing table as she tried to figure out what that terrible feeling she had was. Was it shame? What had she done?

Piper's hand shook as she replaced the bottle on her dresser. Her mind marched her where she didn't want to go. *I kissed Mason Wakefield.*

The thought of that kiss seemed to explode in her body — a memory that left her flushed with desire. Her stomach felt tense, knotted, like it had when he pressed her against the wall. *Oh god.*

Piper breathed deeply and squeezed her eyes shut. The desire inside her gave way to a flood of guilt. She had betrayed Dylan.

She had stepped over the line from harmless thought to damaging action.

Piper pulled the covers over her head. It didn't help. The guilt grew to a storm inside her. She had only been away from home for two weeks and she'd kissed someone else.

Dylan didn't deserve this; he was a loyal and loving boyfriend. And yet, even as she thought that, she could still feel Mason's touch in that laneway, and the way he *wanted* her. Little moments drifted back to her and she tried to shake them out of her head.

After they kissed, Mason had hailed a cab for her. 'We'll talk about this later,' he'd said, his voice low and serious. She'd nodded and buried her head in his chest. When they finally broke away from each other, he'd kissed her again. Tenderly. It had felt like a promise.

She'd floated home. There was no guilt. Not then. When she got in, Gaynor was already in bed. Piper had stripped down to her underwear, dived into bed and let sleep take her.

She wished she could find that oblivion again, but it wasn't going to happen. It was 5 a.m. now and Piper was wide awake, the guilt weighing down on her chest until she found it hard to breathe.

She tiptoed over to the cupboard and pulled out her suitcase. Dylan's song lyrics were still there, inside one of the zip pockets. She took them out and made herself read them. She punished herself with them. Over and over again.

Piper's Song.

A song she didn't deserve.

Piper's phone alarm sounded at 7 a.m., mocking her with the familiar electronic beat, as though it was any other morning and nothing had changed. She switched it off and it sounded again. This time, there was a text on the screen.

I'm out of the office this morning and then I'm in Perth until next Sunday. Can I take you for a drink when I get back? We need to talk. Mason. PS Please.

Piper's heart did cartwheels. It flipped around in her chest and she hugged herself with nervous excitement.

She knew this wasn't the right reaction. It was traitorous. And wrong. She should be so filled with remorse that there was no room for any other emotion.

Her hand hovered over the screen. It would be better to reply quickly, telling him she had a boyfriend as though her response was immediate and unequivocal. As it should be.

But her mind drifted back to his words last night.

That hasn't mattered to me, he'd said. *Until now.* And then, later, *God, I want you, Piper.*

Piper gulped. Her hesitation was horrible. *She* was horrible. There was a knock on Piper's door. It swung open and Gaynor stood there with a coffee in her hand.

'You had a late one. You got home long after me, and I wasn't home until twelve,' Gaynor said, leaning in the doorway. 'Good night?'

'Fine,' Piper said quickly. 'Just ... just a launch thingy.'

'Well, I'm not sure you could say *just* about an *Aspire* party,' Gaynor said. '*Something* must have happened. It always does.'

Piper shrugged, like whatever might have happened was no big deal. But Gaynor's eyebrows were arched.

'What about you, Gaynes?' she countered. 'What did you get up to?'

'Ah, your deflection techniques are still superior,' Gaynor said with a little smirk. 'I'm trying to work on mine. So I'll just say, I had another lovely night.'

'Really?' Piper asked. Come to think of it, Gaynor *had* been out quite a lot lately. 'So, was it ... with somebody?'

'I'm choosing to go dark horse too. No comment,' Gaynor said breezily. 'Shall I put on a crumpet for you?'

'Neigh,' Piper answered, forcing out the joke.

Gaynor's laugh as she closed the door was gorgeous: tinkling and true. The laugh of someone who didn't have a dark secret.

Piper had some work to do to restore her sanity. And it had to begin right now. She picked up her phone and tapped out a message.

What happened last night was a mistake. I should have told you that I have a boyfriend. So sorry. Piper.

Her throat was tight and raw as she pressed send.

18

Mason's head was bursting with way too many thoughts. A meeting with Anita Barnes at 8.30 a.m. was the last place he wanted to be.

'Do you see all those girls out there, all those wannabes?' Anita was demanding.

Mason moved his chair closer to Kara's. Anita Barnes was the most formidable woman Mason had ever come across. Scary, in fact. Next to Anita was Bruce, who was known in the modelling world as *Brutal Bruce*. He was Anita's right-hand man.

'Yes, I see them,' Kara said meekly. The glass door to Anita's office offered the perfect view of about twenty young girls standing at various angles in a queue in the foyer, all of them hoping to be signed to Anita's agency.

'What do you think, Bruce?' Anita urged. 'What's your take on them?'

Bruce stood up and began pointing, his finger moving down the row of aspiring models. 'Too short. Torso too long. Nose too big. Boobs too saggy. A possible. Can see the moustache from here. Legs too dimply. Arse too big. Hair tatty. Too trashy ...'

Anita held up her hand and Bruce stopped speaking.

'They all want what you have, Kara. They all *dream* of being you. Of being where I've got you.'

Kara threw her hands up and then clapped them together. When she was nervous, she gestured a lot. And Anita Barnes on the warpath would make anyone nervous. 'I know,' Kara said. 'And I thank you for that. Truly, Anita. But I also need to be true to myself, and to my partner. It's just ... well ... it's eating away at me. I used to be okay with pretending I wasn't gay. But that was before I met Laurie.' Kara clenched her fists. 'Love makes your soul crawl out from its hiding place,' she said.

'Oh for fuck's sake,' Anita snarled. 'Does your *soul* know that your fan base is seventy per cent male? And that ten per cent of them are homophobic?' She shook her head. 'Of course, some of them might think it's hot. They might like to fantasise about some girl-on-girl action. But none of them are going to be turned on by you making a political statement about being a dyke. We've discussed this before, Kara. You lose even five per cent of your fan base, and you've lost the top position. Do you get that?'

'I get it,' Kara replied, her voice emotional but insistent. 'And

I'm willing to risk it. This whole thing ... me pretending to be what I'm not ...' she looked searchingly at Mason. 'It's been hard on everyone. Laurie doesn't want to do it anymore, and neither do I. I can't keep asking her to keep our relationship a secret. She's over it. She told me she wanted to break up with me at the Cristobel Club that night, Anita. She said she was over all the lies. I lost it. Absolutely lost it.'

'Kara was devastated, Anita,' Mason joined in. 'I was really afraid for her. Laurie's good for Kara. She tries to keep her sober, and she really wants the best for Kara. But the secrecy is killing them both, Anita. You've got to see that!'

Anita Barnes seemed to raise her eyebrows. Or maybe not – it was hard to tell, due to the botox.

'Laurie was so upset about the whole situation,' Kara continued. 'Then, to rub salt in her wounds, the tabloids get a picture of me crying and decide to make it about Mason being an arsehole and breaking up with me. Laurie and I got back together on the proviso that I would come out. It's not fair to Laurie. And it's definitely not fair to Mason.'

Her voice was wobbly, but she was obviously not going to cave. Mason felt proud of her. Laurie was the best thing that had happened to Kara in aeons. She was right to fight for the relationship.

Anita gave a huge, dramatic sigh. 'All right. Bruce, what's the best damage control? If we have to do this, let's do it with a bang, not a whimper.'

Bruce tapped his chin with his index finger — he was wearing yellow nail polish. 'We'll sell the story as a two-page spread to the highest bidder. Complete with photos of you and yours lounging around the eclectic and exotic shared home. You live together?'

'No,' Kara admitted. 'Not all the time, anyway. Laurie doesn't want to move in until —'

'Well, you live together now,' Bruce interrupted. 'You're inseparable. And Kara, I hope your girlfriend isn't butch.'

Mason felt Kara stiffen beside him. Having won the battle, though, she wasn't going to take the bait on this.

'Laurie is beautiful,' she said simply.

'She'd better be,' Anita snapped. 'We will get that happening within the next fortnight. Until then, you two,' she pointed at Mason and Kara, 'are still the golden couple. Got it?'

Kara saved her whooping until they were well clear of Anita's office.

'I'm going to get to be with Laurie. Openly and honestly!' She looked at Mason, flushed with excitement. 'So, now it's time for you to get back into the game, Mase,' she said. 'You must be interested in someone.'

Mason turned away from Kara's stare. 'Not really.'

'Mason, you can't even look at me. There is someone, isn't there?' She put her hands on his face and made him look at her.

Mason shook his head, which was hard to do, given her grip.

There was nothing to tell. *Nothing.* 'Kaz,' he said. 'When I have time for a girlfriend, I'll let you know and you can choose one for me. Preferably one who isn't a lesbian.'

'Oh, you're a dick,' Kara said.

'Bully,' Mason said, rubbing his arm. But he was glad that Kara's love life, at least, had just become a whole lot simpler. 'I don't have time for a girlfriend. Not a real one, anyway.'

19

Wearing another Kara Kingston design didn't help Piper feel any better at work that morning. It felt like espresso martini sweat was seeping through every pore of her body. She kept her sunglasses on as she walked through the foyer, avoiding eye contact with the receptionists and grabbed a copy of the current issue of *Aspire* on the way.

At least there was no-one in the office yet. Piper put her stupid fake bag under her desk and took out her phone to read Mason's reply again.

Thank you for making that clear. I won't bother you again.
Mason.

It was so final.

Piper's hand trembled as she erased the message. What an idiot she'd been to get herself into this situation. It was going to be a real treat, having to see Mason around at work from now on and knowing that she had loved being kissed by him.

She opened up the *Aspire* and flicked through it distractedly.

The photos from the Bojangles shoot were all there. They'd worked out beautifully. Even in the state she was in, Piper was pleased to see that Georgie had a whole page in the bikini shoot, with Kara on the other side of the spread. The two models really complemented each other; Georgie was voluptuous in her red gingham bikini, looking out to the horizon, while Kara, angular in her silver costume, lounged at the shoreline. Georgie would be stoked.

Piper flipped the page. The Aztecs were there, but the pictures of them were much smaller. Immediately, the word *karma* came to mind. She batted it away. Who was *she* to think about karma? If there truly was such a thing, it wouldn't be any good for her. She'd cheated on her boyfriend and fucked things up profoundly. Again.

Oh well, she thought, *at least things can't get much worse.*

Piper flipped the pages to the feature article. This was part of the new direction: Piper read Wendy's three-page feature on plastic surgery. This was definitely not a snippet or a grab – it was incisive, interesting and obviously well researched. It was almost disappointing to get to the end. Especially as she then had to return to her own thoughts.

Piper decided she'd just take a quick look at the horoscopes tucked away near the end of the mag, and then she would try to start her day. But then her eye caught on an article titled 'Sheer Sense.'

Just a few pages from the back cover, there it was — surrounded by some of the photos Piper had sourced. Jennifer Lawrence took prime position in the centre, in a perfect sheer dress. The text was in a box in the upper right-hand corner. Piper's text. As far as Piper could tell, not a word had been changed. Except for two words in bold font at the very end: *Vivian Jacobson*.

Piper wasn't sure how long she'd been sitting there, staring at the article in disbelief, when Lucy came in.

'Piper. What's wrong? You look like shit.'

Piper pointed at the article. 'I wrote this, Lucy,' she said, suddenly snapping out of it. 'Vivian *stole* it.'

She turned to her computer, searching frantically for evidence. The article was gone. There was no trace of it in any of her files. Or in her recycle bin. Slowly, it dawned on her. That's why her computer had been moved the night after she wrote the article. It wasn't the cleaners at all; Vivian must have come in during the night.

She looked at Lucy, tears pricking her eyes. 'You probably don't believe me,' she said softly.

Lucy sighed. She put a finger to her lips in a *shh* gesture. Then she closed the office door, shutting out the growing noise from the hallway. When she came back, she swivelled her chair so it was close to Piper's.

'I believe you,' she whispered. 'I believe you because I know what she's like. I haven't told a soul about this, because I don't have any evidence either. But stuff keeps going missing. After each shoot, I check things off and sign for them. Then I put them in the fashion cupboard. When I'm ready to send them back to the designers, half the time there's something missing.' She paused thoughtfully. 'Vivian is the only other person who has a key to the fashion cupboard, but it looks bad for me, doesn't it? I got an email from Rose the other day, letting me know she's concerned that items have gone missing from other shoots. Basically, if anything else goes missing, I'm cactus.'

'That is so fucked up,' Piper said. 'I'm probably not going to be able to prove what she's done with my article. But you can. You've got to get a camera in the fashion cupboard and then —'

There was a muffled sound coming from the fashion cupboard. Both girls crept towards it, and they opened the sliding doors. Bronwyn was sitting just inside the door, sobbing into a tissue.

'Jesus, what happened, Bron?' Lucy asked.

Bronwyn choked back a sob. 'I showed Vivian my designs,' she said in a low wail. A terrible feeling settled inside Piper's stomach. Bronwyn wiped her eyes. 'She said —,' Bronwyn started, and then had to pause to collect herself. 'She said, *Just because no-one's ever going to understand your designs, it doesn't make you an artist.* Then she called my dresses *try-hard sacks.*' Piper and Lucy exchanged disgusted looks. 'After all this time, she still doesn't know my name,' Bronwyn continued. 'And now this.'

Piper and Lucy waited until Bronwyn calmed down, then they led her back into the office, the three of them pulling their chairs close together for support.

'Wow, you girls look positively *conspiratorial*,' said Vivian, striding into the office.

Piper gasped as she saw the new *Aspire* tucked under Vivian's sharp elbow, folded open to the 'Sheer Sense' article.

Vivian continued as though oblivious. 'I guess it's lucky for you, Piper, that there's no time for gossip in the fashion department.' Her phone rang.

'Hi Rose,' she answered, giving the girls a wink. 'Yes, of course I can.' Rose said something at the other end, and Vivian did a little fake laugh. 'Oh, I couldn't *really* handle it all single-handedly. But thanks.' As she hung up the phone, she clicked her fingers at Bronwyn. 'You. Down to the art department,' she barked.

Piper and Lucy shrugged helplessly as Bronwyn left the office.

'And perhaps you two could see your way to getting some actual work done.' Vivian smiled coolly over her shoulder as she left the room.

20

There wasn't much fanfare when Bronwyn resigned. In fact, Vivian didn't even mention it until Lucy asked where she was. But it was kind of like having a ghost around. The way she'd been mistreated was always on Piper and Lucy's minds.

For the rest of that day, and right through the next week, Piper and Lucy just got on with it. They managed to set up a video camera in the fashion cupboard, and waited to see if anything would go missing after the Stella McCartney shoot. All they could do was hope that Vivian got caught in the trap; at least that would give *some* justice to Bronwyn.

After the initial shock of Vivian stealing her article, Piper realised staying quiet was the only option. If she reported it, Vivian could just as easily accuse Piper of sleeping her way in — and then her career would be over before it had even begun. Would Rose even believe she'd written the article? Would she lose her job?

There were too many risks in taking on Vivian.

Occasionally, she still fantasised about writing and getting features published. It was something, she supposed, to know that Rose considered her writing good enough to publish, even if she hadn't been given credit for it.

And at least Mason hadn't been around. It was just as well, because even the *thought* of him seemed to switch Piper's senses into overdrive. But there wasn't much she could do about that, she decided.

As she packed up on Friday afternoon, getting ready to pick Dylan up from the airport, her senses were kicked into high gear for a different reason. She had been living with the guilt of kissing Mason for a whole week, and it was killing her. She had to tell him. It was the only way.

Piper waited in Arrivals. She couldn't help staring as a couple hugged and kissed like no-one else was there. She felt a stab of envy for them, wishing things could be that simple with Dylan.

Finally, she saw him, all blond, sun-kissed and gorgeous.

His new haircut suited him. It wasn't anything drastic; still very Dylan – saltwater scruffy – but now the ends were neat. He sauntered towards her, a Ripcurl bag slung over his shoulder.

'Babe,' he called. He put the bag down and stared at her. 'Geez, you look … different,' he said. Piper couldn't help smiling.

Other than the hair, Dylan didn't look different at all. He was wearing board shorts and a T-shirt, as usual. His smile was still cheeky. But there was something comforting about how exactly-the-same he was.

'I got a few new bits and pieces,' Piper said, looking down at another of Kara's designs. This time, it was a cream dress with a green-and-pink geometric print. 'I have to dress like this for work,' she explained, feeling a little self-conscious.

'Nice,' Dylan said, but Piper had the impression he wasn't so keen on her new look. When he kissed her, it felt a little cool.

As they got into Gaynor's car, Piper asked him about everything back home.

'Yeah, it's all pretty much the same, babe,' he said. 'Loftie got a new four-wheel drive, so we've been exploring a bit. The band is coming along. Might have a gig lined up soon. Nothing too exciting. What about you? What's been happening at work?'

'Nothing really,' Piper lied. 'It's fine.'

'So, what's the plan?' Dylan asked.

'Well, I thought we'd just go home,' Piper said, feeling the horrible pressure of what she was going to have to tell him when they got there. 'Maybe get some takeaway.'

'Will Gaynor be there?'

'No, she's out tonight.'

'Good,' Dylan said. He reached over and put his hand on her breast. Piper was surprised. It just felt wrong, being groped while driving a car. 'I've missed you, Piper,' he continued. 'Just feel how much.' He pulled her hand down from the steering wheel and put it on his groin. She could definitely feel how much he'd missed her. She was still attracted to him but, at the moment, his erection just felt like another problem she had to deal with.

Piper pulled her hand away slowly, trying to make it just seem like she needed it to steer.

⁓

'Hey, cool apartment,' Dylan said, taking in the space as Piper dropped her keys into her fake bag. 'What about the bedroom? Where is it, babe?'

Piper rolled her eyes, hoping it looked playful.

'Dyl ... we need to talk,' she said. She led him into the lounge room and motioned for him to sit on the couch.

'Geez, Gaynor's really into this animal thing,' he said, stroking the tiger throw as he sat down. He sat with his legs wide apart. Like he normally did, of course, but it seemed impolite for him to sprawl out like that in Gaynor's apartment.

Piper stayed standing. 'Dylan, I don't know how to put this, so I'm just going to say it. Something happened last week.'

Dylan stopped stroking the throw. 'As in?'

Piper breathed deeply. 'I kissed someone, Dyl.'

It was awful, watching his face. Watching how much those four small words thudded into him, like bullets. He put his hand on his heart, as though trying to stem a wound. A tear slid down Piper's cheek.

He said nothing for a moment. 'You kissed someone,' he repeated, as though he needed to let the information sink in. 'God, Piper. You *kissed* someone? I never thought ... I just didn't think you'd do that.' He cleared his throat, his face hardening. 'Was it just a kiss? Or was it more than that?'

Piper knelt down on the carpet in front of him. 'It was just a kiss, Dyl, I swear. I was at a party and the drinks were *really* strong, and I guess I just ... I lost my judgement.'

Dylan put his head in his hands and sat there, for what seemed like an age. The tears slid freely down Piper's cheeks.

'Jesus,' he said. 'Fuck.' When he finally removed his hands, Dylan's face was screwed up with anger. 'This happened *last week*? Why the fuck did you wait till now to tell me? Why couldn't you have just told me on the phone, and I wouldn't have bothered coming all the way down here to see you!'

'I don't know,' said Piper desperately. 'I wanted to tell you to your face. I wanted to talk about it. This doesn't mean it has to end.'

'Doesn't it? Who was it, Piper?' he asked harshly. 'Just some random? Or someone *special*?' He spat the words. 'In fact, don't bother answering that. I probably wouldn't believe whatever you said. And I don't know if it *was* just a kiss, even if you swear it was. It doesn't matter. You *cheated* on me.'

It was horrible, hearing him talk like that. Knowing he was right. 'I'm so sorry,' Piper whispered. 'It will never . . .'

Dylan shook his head. 'I don't want to hear it,' he said. He got up, picked up his Ripcurl bag, slung it over his shoulder and opened the front door. 'I trusted you,' he said.

Piper waited for him to slam the door.

It was worse, somehow, when he closed it silently.

~

'Piper, what's wrong?' Gaynor sat down on the carpet next to her goddaughter.

Piper had no idea how long she'd been there, curled up in the foetal position. 'Gaynes, I've ruined *everything*.' She sat up and the floodgates gushed open. What had been quiet, slinking tears became a waterfall. Her body was racked with sobs.

Gaynor drew Piper to her. She held her, waiting patiently for the sobs to subside. Finally, she cupped her hands on Piper's cheeks and gently tilted her face up. 'Sweetheart. Tell me. Just let it out.'

Piper took a breath. And then she told her everything. About how she'd felt about Mason, right from the beginning. Understanding there was an attraction between them, but feeling like she had it under control. About their kiss and about how guilty she felt. About how Dylan had reacted. Now that she'd finally decided to share her story, it tumbled out of her.

Gaynor listened without interrupting.

'Piper,' she said, when Piper had finally fallen quiet. 'Everyone makes mistakes. Maybe you shouldn't have kissed Mason. But you've been honest about it. A lot of people don't have that kind of integrity. Give Dylan time, let it settle. You might still be able to work things out with him.'

Piper smiled a wobbly smile.

'That's if you *want* to,' Gaynor added. There was just a little bit of squint around Gaynor's eyes.

'Of course I do,' Piper said quickly.

'If he's worth it,' Gaynor added. 'I mean, I haven't actually met him yet, so I'll have to reserve judgement.'

⁓

The sobbing session had exhausted Piper. Still, she slept badly, waking every couple of hours to check her phone to see if Dylan had texted.

He hadn't. Not at 1 a.m. Or 3.25. Or even 4.37.

She finally awoke at around seven to heavy knocking on the front door and Gaynor's footsteps as she went to answer it.

She heard Dylan's voice.

Piper got up and walked into the lounge room.

'Hey,' Dylan said flatly. He looked knackered. As Piper got closer, she could smell alcohol.

'I have to get a few things at the shops,' Gaynor announced.

'Hey,' Piper said softly after Gaynor had left. She searched Dylan's face for clues about what he was thinking, but he wouldn't look at her. 'Where did you go?'

'Out,' he said.

He was making it clear that she didn't have the right to ask him that. Which was fair, she supposed.

'I came back,' Dylan said with a shrug.

Piper almost smiled. That was such a Dylan thing to say. Straight to the point.

'So, what did you ... how do you ...' she tried, but Dylan held his hand up. A stop sign.

'You're not much of a drinker, Piper. I believe you when you say it was just a kiss that happened because you were pissed. That it wasn't with anyone special.' Dylan's eyes narrowed. 'You probably don't even remember it properly, hey?'

The first part was right. She and Mason would never have gone outside together, never have had that moment, if she hadn't been drunk and about to blurt out what she knew about Kara.

But the other part? That she couldn't remember the kiss? That it was with no-one special?

Sure, some of the night was hazy. She couldn't remember what Albert had said at one point that was so funny she'd nearly choked on her drink. She couldn't remember the taxi driver that took her back to Gaynor's. But in that laneway, when she and Mason had kissed, she remembered it. *Every single* part of it.

'So, I've decided I'm going to forgive you,' said Dylan. 'I mean, I'll get there. It might take some time, though. Just, you know, don't do it again, hey?'

Piper stepped towards Dylan. She put her arms around his waist. Even though he was so much taller, he leant down and nestled his face into her shoulder. 'I won't,' she whispered.

His kiss tasted vaguely like beer. But it was a nice kiss.

~

'I've got eggs and bacon and avocado and tomato,' Gaynor chirped when she returned, putting shopping bags on the bench.

Piper gave her a quizzical look. In the time she'd lived with Gaynor, there had never been eggs and bacon and avocado and tomato for breakfast. She wondered whether the point might not have been the actual breakfast, but Gaynor's presence in the apartment to cook it.

'Gosh, I've got a very in-and-out-of-the-house day today,' Gaynor said, as if to confirm Piper's suspicion. 'I'll be coming and going like a crazy thing. Oh, and I've got the cleaner coming too, Piper, and God knows what time she'll be able to get here, so can you make sure your bedroom is ready for her?'

Piper gave Gaynor a frown that Gaynor diligently failed to notice. But part of her was relieved that Gaynes was going to make it impossible for anything to go on between her and Dylan.

I just need to let things settle down, Piper assured herself. *Then*

I'll feel like I've always felt.

'So, what are you two going to get up to?' Gaynor asked, filling a pot with water and popping it on a burner.

'Do you want me to show you around the city?' Piper asked Dylan, who was now sitting on a barstool on the other side of the kitchen bench. He kept pushing the button that made the stool go up and down. Each time, it made a squeaking noise.

'And tonight we've got that thing,' Dylan said, rising upward. 'The party thing with the models. Whatever that is.'

'Seriously, we don't have to go, Dylan,' Piper assured him. 'We could do anything you like.'

'Nah. Yeah. I mean ... I'm fine with it,' Dylan said. He turned around on the stool and Piper could only see his back.

'Nah, yeah, well, that's lovely,' Gaynor said in a too-bright voice, squashing tomatoes down very flat on the frying pan.

Piper gave her a nudge. The mimicked *Nah, yeah* and the poor tomatoes seemed to indicate that Gaynor wasn't exactly enamoured with Dylan. But Piper was. He was her history, her first love, and he had forgiven her.

Piper had no idea what Mason was doing but, with any luck, he'd still be in Perth and wouldn't be able to make it to the party.

Piper texted Kara, asking her if she could have a plus one on her ticket at the door, and received a yes straightaway. It was perfect. She and Dylan would have a great night together, and all this stuff would be behind them.

At last, things could go back to the way they were.

21

'Good to do business,' Mason said, putting the contract for a three-page ongoing advertorial for Prentice Interiors into his briefcase and shaking Emmanuel Prentice's hand.

'Even if you did bust my balls, you did it ever so gently,' Emmanuel replied, doing an impression of their old Harvard lecturer.

'*Seal the deal with a handshake and eye contact,*' Mason said, attempting his own impression of Murphy Sands. '*Tie it up with a bloody bow.*'

Emmanuel grinned. He really did look happy.

'You did all right, Manny,' Mason said. 'It's a good deal. For *Aspire* and for Prentice.'

'Well, at least I *timed* it well for Friday night drinks,' Emmanuel said, pouring two very large scotches from the bar in his office. He plonked one in front of Mason.

'Bit of a change from New York, eh?' Emmanuel motioned to the window with a beach view that seemed to go on forever.

'Yeah,' Mason agreed. The scotch tasted good; it had a mellow complexity and a smoky flavour. 'So, how do you feel about coming back home?'

'Love it,' Emmanuel replied. 'I get a surf in before work. I'm earning good money. What's not to like?'

'What about going back into the family business?' Mason asked.

'It's what I always wanted, Wakefield,' Emmanuel said. 'But, as far as I remember, it wasn't what *you* wanted.'

'I needed to come home, to help straighten out Dad's business for a while.' Mason said. 'It won't be forever.'

'You got offered something in Silicon Valley, didn't you?'

Mason nodded. 'Google.'

'Nice,' said Emmanuel. 'Sorry it didn't work out. But Australia's not such a bad place to be. And, listen, I've landed on a bit of inside goss. Apparently Oracle is planning to open in Australia, and Melbourne seems to be the hot favourite. Word is they're hunting down a director of business development, and you'd be perfect, Wakefield – since you're a ball-breaking hardarse.'

Mason was definitely listening. The job he'd been offered in Silicon Valley wasn't a director's position; it was just working as an analyst. Mason knew that Oracle's headquarters were in Redwood,

California, and that the company had a big slice of the pie in computer software and hardware. A director's role with them sounded more like a giant leap than a stepping stone. He could have seriously considered it if his dad was well enough to run *Aspire* again. And if things had turned out differently with Piper.

Mason mentally ran through the message Piper had sent him. The one he'd erased from his phone, but not from his mind.

What happened last night was a mistake. I should have told you I have a boyfriend. So sorry. Piper.

She had a boyfriend. He was nothing but a mistake to her.

But he couldn't stop thinking of her lips against his. Her body pressing back into his.

Mason tapped his temples, trying to redirect his stupid brain. He should never have let down his guard. Let her under his skin. He had known better and he'd still gone and kissed her. That was his mistake.

'Jeez, you're wandering, mate,' Emmanuel said, pouring a third scotch. 'Email me your CV now, before you disappear. I'll pass it on to my mates. Just see how things land, Wakefield.'

⌒

Mason woke up in his hotel room on Saturday morning and checked his phone. There was a message from his dad on the screen.

How did you go with Prentice Junior? Come over as soon as you arrive. Have something to tell you.

He looked at the message again. Everything to do with his dad triggered worries lately. The first part of the text was promising; his dad hadn't asked an *Aspire*-related question for a long time. But the second was troubling. Some other issue may have unfolded in the ex-wife disaster.

Mason's ticket was booked for the next day. He'd planned to take the day to check out Perth, to see how the mining boom was playing out in other industries. So far, the domino effect was obvious from the inflated price he'd had to pay for this very ordinary hotel room, but he wondered about other businesses.

Then he pictured his dad, lying on the couch in his pyjamas, miserable, and went online to change his flight.

⁓

Mason put his key in the door of his dad's house, but before he could open it himself his dad was there. He noticed with surprise that Patrick's eyes were clear, for the first time in ages. His shirt and trousers were clean and crisp. And, despite it being 6 o'clock on a Saturday night, there was no scotch bottle in sight.

'You look good, Dad,' Mason said, with a relieved smile.

'Well, I guess I've been shocked back into the land of the living,' Patrick replied. He strode to the lounge room and motioned for Mason to sit down.

'There's been a bit of drama at the *Aspire* headquarters,' he said. 'It turns out, we've caught a thief.'

'Lucy?' Mason asked.

'No. Lucy was the detective on this one,' Patrick replied. Even though the news wasn't good, Mason had the distinct sense that his dad was enjoying being back on deck.

'So, it happened like this,' Patrick continued. 'Rose got a call from the alarm company last night for an out-of-hours open. When she got there to check things out, she saw Vivian's car pull out from the car park. She supposed Vivian had forgotten something, or had some urgent work to do. But since things had gone missing from the fashion cupboard lately, she wasn't comfortable about the whole thing.'

Mason nodded and his father continued animatedly. 'So she called Vivian's assistant, Lucy someone. Turns out that Lucy had her own suspicions, and she'd set up a video camera in there.'

'That's pretty enterprising,' Mason said.

Patrick got up and turned on the TV. Onto the screen flickered an image of the fashion cupboard, with Vivian striding in.

She obviously knew exactly what she was after. Mason watched as she rifled through the racks. When she exited, it was with a ten thousand-dollar Givenchy gown.

'Jesus,' Mason said. 'She's been pointing the finger at Lucy. And I was pretty close to accepting that was the case, despite Rose having one of her *feelings* that it wasn't right.'

Patrick switched off the TV. 'Since you were in Perth, Rose and Lucy came over here to tell me in person. And, son, you gotta know by now that Rose's *feelings* are ninety-nine per cent on the mark.'

Mason tilted his head. 'What would we do without Rose?' he said gratefully.

'Lucy's a good egg, too,' replied Patrick. 'It turns out that Vivian Jacobson is a thief in more ways than one. Lucy ended up telling me that Vivian also took the credit for an article by some junior in their office, and passed it off as her own. Piper something?'

Mason braced himself at the mention of her name. Vivian may have been a thief, but she was not an idiot. The black leather-and-lace Givenchy gown she had stolen was hugely valuable, as were most of the other items that had gone 'missing'. Piper obviously had talent if Vivian wanted to steal her work. *Talent stacked on instinct stacked on wit stacked on charm stacked on . . .*

'So, Mason, I guess I've got a busy Monday morning coming up,' Patrick said, thankfully interrupting the thoughts in Mason's head. 'A sacking and a reshuffle are in order.'

'I guess we have,' Mason agreed, but already he knew what his father was getting at.

'Not *we*, Mason,' Patrick corrected. 'You've done enough. You've done an excellent job getting this company back on its feet, and I'm so proud you.' He clapped his hand on his son's shoulder. 'You've always looked out for me. But now you need to get on with your own life. I'll be fine.'

Mason tilted his head to the side. 'So, how are you feeling about all the Abigail stuff?'

'Abigail who?' said Patrick wryly. And though there was still sadness, the light in his eyes was stable.

Mason was glad he'd given Emmanuel Prentice his CV. Manny was very well connected, and his information would be good. Now, he would just wait and see what happened with Oracle. At least it felt like *some* things were on the move. 'Welcome back, Dad.'

When Mason got to The Texan, security guards whisked him through the VIP entrance, past the paparazzi and people queuing up to get inside the club. He was delivered to Kara who met him with a beaming smile and hands behind her back, like she was hiding something.

'I'm so glad you could come, Mase,' she said, planting a kiss on his cheek and pulling him into a corner. From behind her back, Kara produced the latest *Who* magazine, open to a double-page spread.

Mason looked at the pictures of Kara and Laurie. The lovebirds in the lounge room. The lovebirds by the pool. Not a terribly original shoot, but it definitely did the job. Mason read aloud from the article.

Sapphic Style

Kara Kingston has never been one to do things by halves.

Coming out publicly in an exclusive with Who, Kara tells of her love for DJ Laurie Anderson and of the home they share.

'I've been doing battle with myself,' Kara confides. 'With the

unconditional support and forward-thinking of my agent, Anita Barnes, I finally feel like I can expose my true identity.'

Exposing her true identity looks good on Kara Kingston. Today, she's wearing a white halter-neck Prada dress that screams casual chic. Her dark hair is cropped short to highlight her famous cheekbones. Sitting in the lounge room, which boasts an eclectic mix of sharply angled modular furniture, white tiles and Laurie's DJ equipment, her smile is dazzling. As Laurie enters the room, the wattage rises even higher.

'I hope my fans will be able to accept me and to help celebrate,' Kara adds.

Changing into a silver string Hermes bikini and a flowing toga to walk pensively around her pool, Kara Kingston is pure goddess. Only now does this reporter realise that she's more beautiful today, in the flesh, than even as an airbrushed cover girl of Sports Illustrated.

It must be love.

Whatever it is, Kara's fans will love it.

Mason gave Kara a hug.

'Well, that's great, oh goddess, with a supportive, forward-thinking agent,' he teased.

Kara rolled up the magazine and flicked him on the arm with it.

'You're officially off the hook, Mase,' she said. 'So, whatcha gonna do with that?'

Everything was bigger and better in The Texan. Kara led Mason through throngs of people on the vast dance floor as Larry took his post by the bar, surveying the room. Many of the partiers were sipping the club's famous cocktail, Texas Tea, through elongated straws that wound through giant plastic bubble glasses. A light show played around the space, blinking and spilling colour everywhere as the crowd moved to the music. Laurie was set up with her decks on stage, a giant, floor-to-ceiling lava lamp bubbled green and gold behind her.

'Isn't Laurie just the best?' Kara yelled into Mason's ear.

Mason nodded. It had been a long time since he'd seen her so happy. He'd witnessed quite a few arguments between Kara and Laurie, but every one of them was to do with the same thing. Now that Kara was out, there was absolutely no reason to argue anymore. He watched as Kara took a sip of her clear drink.

'Water,' Kara said, putting the glass under Mason's nose for a smell test. 'It's this new fad Laurie introduced me to.'

Mason smiled. *Sobriety* looked good on Kara.

'It's so great to see you like this,' Mason yelled, but his attempt to communicate with Kara was lost in the swell of music. Then, suddenly, he was grabbed by both arms.

'Mason Wakefield. Now I'm *really* glad I came here tonight.' The dark-haired beauty on his right dug her fingers into Mason's arms. '*Obviously*, I do get asked to loads of events. People are always hassling me. It's all, *Xena, please come here, Xena, please go there*. But tonight, I *chose* to come to The Texan.'

Xena was a walking self-marketing machine. The way she mentioned her name so often was clearly designed to make it stick in his mind. And it *was* sticking, but probably not in the way she'd wanted it to. Mason tried to back away, but he was sandwiched by another very similar-looking girl.

'What other offers did you have?' the other girl asked.

'So, *obviously* you guys aren't together anymore,' Xena ignored her, patting Mason's arm suggestively. 'I saw the *Who* article today.'

Kara's smirk was evil. 'No, ladies, he's all yours.'

Mason glared at her.

'Actually,' Kara relented, taking pity as the girls pawed Mason like he was a piece of meat, 'I'm going to borrow him for a little while. But he'll *definitely* be free later.'

One of the girls took out her mobile phone. Within seconds, she had taken several photos of herself and Mason.

'Come back soon, Mason,' the girls said in unison as Kara pulled him up some stairs beside the stage.

Mason breathed a sigh of relief as he escaped their clutches. 'Jesus, do *I* need a bodyguard?' he joked as they reached a booth up above the stage. It was much quieter there. Just Kara and a few friends standing around or lounging on padded velvet couches. A waiter poured Moet into tall crystal glasses and Mason took a long, cool sip.

'Mason, this is Georgie,' Kara said.

'Hi Georgie, how do you know Kara?' he began politely.

'Oh, I met Kara on the Bojangles shoot and ...' Mason

nodded, pretending to listen as Georgie continued talking. But he wasn't listening at all. Because across the room, there was Piper.

If he didn't need to be there for Kara, he would have walked straight out of there. Or maybe he would have stopped to give Piper a serve. He'd been told several times that he could be harsh. Well, he'd like to be a little bit harsh with Piper Bancroft. He wasn't going to be anyone's *mistake*.

Even if that someone made his heart race and every nerve jump to the surface of his skin.

Mason took a deep breath to calm himself. Christ, what was *wrong* with him? Obviously Piper didn't give a flying fuck about what had happened between them. For her, it was just a misplaced snog at a work function. There was no point being angry with her because she didn't feel the same as he felt. But there it was. Anger.

Anger mixed with lust or love or whatever the fuck is going on.

She was wearing black silk pants and a dusty-pink beaded singlet that hugged her breasts. Her hair was swept up in a ponytail.

With her was a tall, surfie-looking guy with shaggy blonde hair. He looked like he'd been recently scrubbed and forced into a white shirt and black pants.

The boyfriend.

Mason shook his head. It was good for him to actually see the boyfriend. To see clear evidence that Piper Bancroft was a cheat. He tried to tell himself that she wasn't worth all the shit he was putting himself through, but it was sadness, more than anything else, that he felt.

Mason gave Piper a quick dismissive nod. He turned back to Georgie, feeling the thumping music beat in time with the thud of his heart.

Then from below came the DJ's voice. 'As DJ at The Texan, sometimes I get to shamelessly promote the songs that resonate for me and who I play them for. Tonight . . . ' there was a pause as Laurie collected herself, 'I would like to dedicate a song to my lover and my best friend.' She waited. A hush came over the audience.

'Love makes your soul crawl out from its hiding place,' she said, the same words Kara had used with Anita Barnes. 'Kara Kingston . . . here's to you. Here's to us.' As soon as she said that, the bubbling lava lamp changed from green to red. Liquid red love hearts floated around, floor to ceiling. Kara leant over the balcony, her glass raised. The crowd clapped and cheered as a song pumped into the air.

Despite himself, Mason looked over at Piper.

She was looking right at him. 'I'm sorry,' she mouthed.

Mason ripped his eyes away. He sat on one of the couches and tried to find his feelings as Georgie chattered.

⌐

'Are you okay, Mase? You look kind of shaken,' Kara said, a little later, coming to sit next to Mason on the couch. Georgie had found someone else to chat with.

Piper had gone to dance, leaving her jacket on the back of a seat. Her boyfriend was still there. Mason watched him refuse an offer of champagne from the waiter and ask her for a beer.

'I'm fine,' Mason lied.

But Kara was having none of it. 'You seemed fine until . . . ' she lowered her voice to a whisper. 'Mason, you seemed fine until you caught sight of *Piper*. Oh my god. You're gone, aren't you, Wakefield?' she said, triumphant. 'Smitten.'

'I never said that,' Mason protested.

'You didn't need to,' Kara whispered. 'Poor Mase. And she's got a boyfriend. That sucks.'

'Okay, I do like her,' Mason conceded. 'But it's just a flesh wound.'

Kara smiled, which was what Mason had wanted from the Monty Python joke. She was floating high on the first show of public approval, on the freedom of finally being herself. Mason wasn't going to ruin that for her, no matter how he felt.

'Okay,' Kara continued, 'but I want to talk to you about this later.'

Mason was glad when Kara was pulled away by a well-wisher. A moment alone was just what he needed.

Then Piper's boyfriend sat next to him on the couch. He spread his legs wide. 'I'm Dylan,' he said.

His handshake was firm, with hands calloused by manual labour. Hands that had touched Piper Bancroft. Mason felt like a wild animal, pretending to be tame.

'Can you believe that about Kara Kingston?' the boyfriend continued, shaking his head. 'I mean, it's pretty full-on. Her and that DJ, hey? Dunno if it's cool or a waste. Kind of depends how you think about it.'

Mason had the feeling that Dylan *was* thinking about it. Right then. 'Yes, well, each to their own,' he replied coldly.

'Yeah, true that,' Dylan said, ignoring the vibe Mason put out. He took his phone out of his pocket and seemed to commandeer even more space on the couch.

Mason shifted a little further away. As he glanced sideways, he noticed there was a photo on Dylan's screen. From where he sat, it looked like it was of a girl on a beach at night. Flames from a bonfire lit the foreground.

Mason watched as Dylan gave it a quick glance and erased it. He seemed keen to do it properly, checking twice that the image was gone. Then he shoved the phone back in his pocket. Mason could have sworn that he looked guilty.

'Dylan. OMG. How good was last night?'

Mason turned to see Xena and her friend standing on the top stair of the booth.

'Two hot guys on one couch,' Xena exclaimed. Then she reduced her voice to a hoarse whisper. 'Wanna come and have a line, boys? Dylan, you'll *love* it. It's the same stuff as last night,' she added sexily. Obviously they'd all been partying the night before. And maybe that was what Piper Bancroft was, deep down, despite her intelligence. A party girl. A random kisser.

Mason shook his head. The last thing he wanted to do was to party with those girls and Dylan.

But Dylan looked like he was seriously considering the offer. 'Hey, mate,' he said to Mason, 'I think Piper's dancing, but if she comes back, can you just tell her I'll be ten minutes?'

Mason shrugged, bristling at being called Dylan's *mate*. It seemed like he was being asked to leave out the detail of where Dylan was going to be for that ten minutes and who he was going to be with.

Dylan took the shrug as agreement, and soon the girls flanked him and led him down the stairs.

As soon as they'd gone, Mason felt something vibrate on the couch next to him. Dylan's phone. There was no-one else up in the loft at the moment, so Mason picked it up. He guessed he'd have to go and find Dylan before he left the club. It wouldn't be hard, since he'd most likely be in the toilets.

'Mason?' Piper stood at the top of the stairs. Her hair was tousled and her face flushed from dancing. She looked gorgeous. His eyes were locked on her as she walked towards him.

Mason stood up. 'Your *boyfriend* wanted me to tell you he'll be back in ten minutes,' he said. Despite his intentions of keeping himself controlled, he couldn't keep the tremor of emotion from his voice.

He walked past Piper, over to the stairs. He had to get out of there. Now. But there was her hand. On his arm. He turned around.

'I wanted to tell you in person that I'm sorry,' Piper breathed. 'I need to explain. Well, as much as I *can* explain.' She paused. 'Dylan and I have been going out for quite a while. We've always been faithful to each other. What happened with you . . . well . . . that wasn't the way I act. It was like I couldn't help it. That's what's so weird.' She faltered, obviously trying to say something that might make sense. To herself and to him. 'I just . . . I'm just . . . God. It's really confusing.' Her words floated in the space between them.

It was like she couldn't help it. The lump of anger inside Mason's chest melted. In a way, it was harder without it. At least the anger had provided a bit of protection; now, he couldn't help drinking in the sight of her.

'Dylan has forgiven me,' Piper said softly. 'Or, he's in the *process* of forgiving me. It won't be easy. He didn't even come home last night, but I suppose that's part of the process. Anyway, I just needed the time to think about what's gone on. How I've hurt him.'

Mason bit his lip. All the resistance he'd been able to summon was gone now. Piper hadn't been out partying with those models and her boyfriend last night. She'd been reflecting on what had happened between them.

God, he'd never stopped reflecting on that. He remembered the taste of her. And he wanted her, so badly it hurt.

He thought of the photo on Dylan's phone. Thought of Dylan, down there right now snorting coke with Xena and her friend. But this was Piper's call. It didn't matter if their kiss had been perfect.

It didn't matter that he'd felt his whole body responding to her. Piper had chosen Dylan.

Now, Mason had to get away from her. And stay away. There were people coming up the stairs now. Piper looked even more conflicted than before. But Mason didn't want to talk anymore.

It was time to walk away. To get on with his own life, without the magazine. Without Piper Bancroft.

He leant in close to her, so he could whisper in her ear, and breathe her in, one last time. 'It's okay, Piper,' he murmured. 'Whatever it was between us, it's over.' Already, in his mind, he was out the door of this stupid club.

Just before he descended the stairs, he remembered he still had Dylan's phone in his hand, and slipped it into the pocket of Piper's jacket.

22

Piper grabbed her jacket from the back of the chair. The Texan seemed strangely airless and dull since Mason had left, like he'd taken all the oxygen with him. She felt empty inside, too. She thought of his words.

Whatever it was, it's over.

She looked over the edge of the balcony. In among the pulsating throng she saw Dylan dancing with Xena and Petal — it looked like he might be having a bit too much fun. But she wasn't really in a position to judge him; not after what she'd put him through.

Maybe she just needed to go outside for a bit.

The woman on the door stamped her hand so she could get back inside. Piper looked at it and smiled weakly. It was a heart-shaped stamp that read *Laurie Anderson and Kara Kingston. Big Love at The Texan.*

It was nice that some people, at least, had their love lives sorted.

The night air was bracing. Piper breathed deeply, but she couldn't shake the hollow feeling in her chest. The queue to get into The Texan was still long, as though it was the place people just *had* to be. But Piper didn't want to be there anymore.

Outside, cold air swirled around her, whipping her hair around. Piper dug down in her jacket pockets for warmth. Her right hand came across something hard. She pulled it out.

Piper's own phone was in her bag. It certainly wasn't like Dylan to put his phone in her pocket, but Piper could tell by the crack along the back that it was his.

She turned it over to the front.

On the screen, there was a message waiting. Piper saw it was a photo of . . . Leanne? Her hairdresser?

Piper blinked. She clicked on the message and looked again. It was a selfie of Leanne. Her hair was wet, like she'd just got out of the shower, and her lips were puckered, as though she were sending a kiss. In front of her chest, she held a piece of paper with writing on it.

Piper felt a sense of foreboding as she zoomed in on the photo. Now she could see the print.

Leanne's Song

Before I met you baby,
life was coloured grey.
There wasn't any loving in my
ordinary day.
Your blue eyes make my heart pump,
it's you that I adore.
If you tell me that you love me,
I'll say I love you more.
Now life is bright and breezy,
you're my one best score.
When you tell me that you love me,
girl, just know I love you more.

The wind roared around her now, but the roar growing inside her was stronger, fiercer.

Two words. He'd only changed *two words*.

But Piper had several for him.

She strode back into The Texan.

Piper wove her way through the crowd on the dance floor. Dylan was right where she'd seen him last. His arms were wound around Xena and Petal's waists, but he was still managing to do his jerky, all-over-the-shop dance moves. She used to think it was cute.

Not anymore.

As he spotted Piper, he dropped both arms. Xena and Petal kept dancing around him, keeping him in the centre.

'Hey babe, where you been?' he said into the din.

In answer, Piper held up the phone. Dylan stopped moving. Piper pointed to the door and started walking.

When they found a spot outside to be alone, Piper thrust his phone into his hand. '"Leanne's Song", hey?' she demanded. 'How very strange, Dyl. I recognise that song. I thought it was called "Piper's Song".'

Dylan looked at the screen, then put the phone in his pocket. He rubbed his arms, staving off the cold. Staving off his response.

Piper waited. She wasn't going to help him.

'Aw, come on, babe,' he said finally. 'I *wrote* it for you.'

'Did you?' Piper said quickly. 'I'm beginning to wonder whether you just recycled it for me after you'd given it to someone else.'

'No, seriously babe.' There was an expression of relief on Dylan's face, as though she'd given him a lifeline. Piper felt like strangling him with it. 'Babe, I promise, I wrote the song for you. I just . . . well . . . I just ended up giving it to Leanne. You know, like, as a favour.'

'Well, I'm glad you didn't put too much effort into altering it for her,' Piper seethed.

As she spoke, she remembered hearing the Beyoncé track in the background when she'd rung Dylan at his place. She remembered the female voice in his office when she'd been waiting for him to book the flight to Melbourne. She remembered Ally, straining and serious, letting her know Dylan's car was out the front of Leanne's house. How she'd made him her first priority when she should have been studying, despite her mum's constant protests. How that decision had changed her life.

She'd been a fool.

'So, what could have made you decide to give her the song?' Piper quizzed.

Dylan scuffed his shoe on the ground.

'You've been with her, haven't you?'

'Well . . . yeah . . . kind of,' he said slowly. 'But, you know, like, it wasn't anything big. Like, you're the one, Piper. Leanne was just kind of . . . well, she was just sort of *there*.'

'How far did you go?' Piper asked. She purposely kept her voice soft now. She didn't want to scare him away from telling the truth. God knew, she needed to hear it. Finally.

'Aw, babe, you know how it is with chicks like that. Just, you know, we kind of . . . a few times here and there . . . you know.'

Piper did know. If Dylan hadn't had sex with Leanne, he would definitely be defending himself now.

'So, it was just convenient?' Piper asked. She felt vaguely conscious of luring him into a trap.

Dylan nodded. 'Yeah, well, that's it, babe,' he said, grasping at the excuse she'd flung his way. 'It's just, you know, like a guy thing. Like, you were away and all . . . ' Dylan suddenly snapped his head up.

'You did it too, Piper,' he said accusingly.

Piper sighed. 'Dylan, I *told* you about what I did,' she said. 'You had a chance to tell me too, but you didn't take it.' She felt tears spring to her eyes. 'You were going to keep going like that. You were going to twist what I'd done and use it against me, when you'd actually done worse yourself.'

Dylan stepped towards her and put his hands on her shoulders. They felt heavy.

'Yeah. I guess that's not right,' he admitted. He looked her in the eyes. 'Look, Piper. I reacted like that because I honestly don't like the idea of you being with someone else. I'm a bloke. And I've got *urges*; it's just the way it is. It's not like I'm going to fall for Leanne or anything like that. But you, you have this thing where you'd probably end up overanalysing everything. You could end up convincing yourself that a random kiss was something more.' He paused. 'You'd probably just get all confused.'

Piper breathed in. That last bit was true. She was already confused. She didn't say anything. She could almost see Dylan looking for words to sell his action plan.

'The thing is,' he continued, searching for words to press home his point, '*essentially*, I'm yours. The other stuff doesn't matter.'

Piper took a step backwards, shrugging her shoulders free. 'So, wait, let me get this straight,' she said. '*You* can be with other people, but *I* should stay faithful to you.'

'I didn't mean it like that,' Dylan said defensively.

Piper shook her head. Just then, Xena and Petal appeared at

the doorway of the club.

'How long are you going to be, Dylan?' Xena called. 'We're about to chop up again.'

Piper looked at the girls. Did they even know Dylan was supposed to be with her? They probably wouldn't care even if they did. She could feel Dylan's desire to go back inside with the two beautiful, empty girls and get wasted.

And suddenly, Piper knew. She didn't want to be part of any of it. 'Dylan, it's over,' she said.

Dylan stared at her. 'You can't mean that, babe.'

'Yes, I can,' Piper replied firmly. 'You slept with another girl, and you hid it from me. And you made me feel like shit for doing something that wasn't nearly as bad.'

Dylan hung his head, as though he finally felt some shame. Tears sprang from his reddened eyes. 'Babe, you and me . . . we're *it* . . . ' he fumbled desperately.

'It's over, Dyl. It's so over.' She didn't need to *analyse* this. Her feelings were clear. 'I'll make sure your stuff gets back to Mission Beach.' She didn't care how much it would cost to send his luggage home. She just didn't want to see him again.

⁓

Piper stood alone outside The Texan and called Gaynor.

'Hi, love, how are you? I only just got home,' Gaynor said. Piper could hear her keys jangling.

'Gaynes,' she said softly, 'can you do me a favour? Can you come and pick me up?'

Gaynor's keys stopped jangling.

'Oh sweetheart,' she said. 'Of course I can. But why? What happened?'

Piper could hear the squeaking sound the leather couch made when you sat on it. She knew that Gaynor would be there, listening, for as long as Piper wanted. That was how it was with Gaynes. Piper wished she'd realised that earlier.

'I just broke up with Dylan,' Piper said, trying to keep the tears in. 'After all that drama last night, it turns out that he's been seeing someone else.' She didn't mention how she found out, and she didn't say anything about the song. That bit was too humiliating.

Piper could hear Gaynor exhaling slowly before she spoke. Gaynes wasn't the type for platitudes, and Piper knew, instinctively, that Gaynor wouldn't be sorry about the breakup.

'So, sweetheart, the important thing is that you're okay. Are you?' she asked.

Piper looked up at the sky. The moon was a sliver. One day, it would be full again. She let a few tears slip down her cheek.

'I'm fine, actually,' she said. And, in saying it, she knew it was true. She was fine.

'You sound fine,' Gaynor confirmed. 'But listen, Piper, where are you? I'll be right there.'

'I cannot believe you even own *one*, Gaynes, let alone two. So stylish!'

'Well, they were two-for-one,' Gaynor replied. 'And they're just for emergencies. Anyway, this one is not your ordinary Snuggie. It's leopard-print microplush, after all.' She smoothed the fabric covering her body as though it was the most luxurious fabric in the world.

'Ah, that's fine then,' Piper replied. She definitely felt ridiculous, sitting on Gaynor's couch in what was, bottom line, a blanket with sleeves. But, she had to admit, there was something extra comforting about being cocooned like this. Plus, she'd been able to use her hands to set up a 3 a.m. Skype call with Ally and Sarah.

Both of them looked extremely bed-heady. Sarah was pretty vague, like she was still half-asleep. But they were there.

Such reliable friends, Piper thought, *always in my corner.*

'Guess I've been a bit of an ostrich,' Piper said to the screen, as Gaynor handed her a cup of tea and went back into the kitchen. 'I mean, Mum was always anti-Dylan, but I was pretty sure that was just her snobby side coming out. But I should have listened to you, Ally, when you told me about Dylan's car being at Leanne's place.'

Ally shook her head. 'We should have pulled your head out of the sand a bit better,' she said.

'Yeah, like with an excavator,' Sarah joined in.

'But we didn't really know anything,' Ally said. 'We only *suspected* he was a dog. I guess you had to put all the pieces together and figure it out. You've always been good at that sort of thing.'

'You think?' Piper asked. It was strange, but even with all the angst going on inside her, it pleased her to hear that.

'We *know*,' Sarah replied.

Piper shook her head. 'I suppose it's harder to be objective when you're involved,' she said. 'And maybe he is a dog, but I guess we both made mistakes.'

'You faced up to yours, Piper,' Ally asserted, echoing Gaynor's sentiments. 'He's just . . . well, I think he's actually just really immature.'

As soon as Ally said that last word, Piper thought about Mason. That was it, really. He was mature in a way that Dylan couldn't be. He was a man, rather than a boy. But her chances with him were shot. In a way, she was glad her best friends had never met him, that their thoughts on him were sketchy. Because she was going to have to erase him from her mind. Piper reached out a Snuggied arm for a tissue. 'I'm okay, girls. Truly,' she said, wiping her teary face. 'It's just a flesh wound.'

Ally and Sarah both smiled. The three of them were probably the only people under forty who understood the Monty Python joke.

'Want us to come down?' Ally asked after a moment. 'We could get there for a few days before uni starts.'

Piper shook her head. It was gorgeous of Ally to offer, but they couldn't really afford a trip to Melbourne at the moment.

Piper knew that they were there for her. A bit of physical distance couldn't change that.

Besides, there was something she wanted to focus on. Not just her work at *Aspire*, but her long-term goals. Maybe she could beg to help Wendy out somehow, even after her regular work hours?

'Thanks, but no,' Piper said. 'I'm not going to let all this go against me. I've got work, but I also want to get a new folio together.'

'Go girl,' Sarah said. 'So, you're going to try to get into the creative writing course again?'

'I think there's been a bit of a detour away from that idea,' Piper said. As she was saying it, she knew it was right. It was as though loads of things had conspired to get her to this point. It just seemed to make sense.

'I'm going get my shit together and apply for journalism,' she announced.

23

'You've got a busy Monday ahead of you,' Vivian said as she handed Piper a list of jobs. Piper held in a sigh: more pickups, more deliveries, data entry and confirmation of the catering requirements for a Thakoon shoot.

'And Lucy, make sure that there isn't a single stuff-up with the Georg Jensen hand models. The last girl Anita Barnes sent had a freaking wart on her ring finger.'

It was weird how Lucy seemed to stare Vivian down, rather than looking away as usual. It actually made Piper pause rather than get on with her work.

'As in *now*, girls,' Vivian said, clicking her fingers.

At that moment, Patrick Wakefield entered the office. Piper

knew who it was straightaway. He was so like Mason, though his hair was grey.

'Vivian,' he said. His voice was deep and even, but there was no mistaking the tone. This was serious. 'My office. As in *now*.'

As soon as they'd gone, Lucy turned to Piper. 'Ding, dong the witch is dead,' she squealed.

'What's going on?' Piper asked, in shock.

'Do I have news for you,' Lucy said, wheeling her chair over.

~

'I know it was you two,' Vivian hissed, standing in the doorway of the office, clutching a hurriedly packed box in her claw-like hands. 'You're the ones who sold me out.'

Lucy and Piper looked at each other and exchanged a nervous smile. A sacked Vivian was a much less venomous one – but she was still a snake.

'Christ, the *cops* are at my house. Going through my things!' Vivian ranted.

'Well, if they are *your* things,' Lucy said, 'then it won't be a problem.'

'And you,' Vivian said, spinning to glare at Piper. 'You little slut. I know what you're playing at. After all I've done for you!'

Piper raised her eyebrow. 'Like stealing my article?' she asked. 'Thanks for that.'

'You girls are nothing,' Vivian spat. 'You haven't learnt a single fucking thing from me.'

Lucy and Piper looked at each other. This time, their smiles were defiant.

'Bye bye from Bronwyn, Viv,' Lucy called. 'And please be assured that we *have* learnt something from you.'

And, without even having planned it, Piper and Lucy both clicked their fingers and pointed to the door.

⁓

It was mid-morning and Piper was working through some data entry when she got a call to see Rose in her office.

As usual, Rose seemed to be doing a hundred things at once and making it look effortless. There were masses of new photos on her desk, and Bruno was nestling in a pile of pink chiffon at her feet.

'Well. Congratulations on your "Sheer Sense" article, Piper.' She sat down and leant back in her chair. 'I *knew* something good would come out of having you at *Aspire*,' she said kindly. 'It's in your energy.'

Piper smiled, remembering the first time she'd been in that office. It seemed so long ago, after all that had happened. But Piper vividly recalled Rose telling Vivian, *I have a good feeling about her.* And, despite not really believing in all that spooky stuff, Piper appreciated the goodwill Rose emanated.

'Thanks, Rose,' she began.

But Rose was already moving on. 'I think your skills might extend beyond the tasks you're doing at the moment. How would you feel about joining Wendy and Lawrence in features?'

24

'That's a really good start, Piper,' Wendy said, looking over Piper's shoulder.

Piper had been moved into the features office just up the hall, with a small window that showed just enough of the outside to remind Piper that the world still existed. Lawrence often worked at home, so Piper was mainly guided by Wendy.

'But maybe reshuffle the paragraphs so that part in the middle,' she pointed at the screen, 'becomes the intro. Oh, and delete half the adjectives and pare it back until only the bare bones remain. It will hit harder that way.'

Very soon after she'd started reporting to Wendy and Lawrence, Piper had realised what a tough gig it was. But Wendy's management style wasn't bossy, like Vivian's. She was more carrot than stick.

Piper's original idea of throwing herself into building up her folio after the break-up with Dylan seemed amusing now. Working hard wasn't optional with Wendy; it was simply expected. So far, Rose and Patrick Wakefield hadn't needed to freelance out any *Aspire* articles, because Wendy was willing and able to write as much as was asked of her. And whatever she required of herself, she also expected of Piper. Piper couldn't count how many dinners she'd eaten in front of her computer screen. Although she did love the work, Piper sometimes fantasised about going back to her old role for a rest.

When Wendy left the office to interview a prison warden for the next month's feature, Piper leant back in her chair. She took some deep breaths to refresh her over-stimulated mind.

The other fantasies, the ones that included Mason Wakefield, were thankfully abating. When his father came back to work, Mason had disappeared from *Aspire* altogether.

As if summoned by her thoughts, Patrick Wakefield knocked on her office door.

'Hello, Piper, I'm looking for Wendy,' he said. Piper liked his manner. For a boss, he was very approachable, he knew everyone's names and what their roles were. To top it all off, he was a great magazine man: this month's *Aspire* was one Piper would have bought herself. Still, his resemblance to Mason made her a bit edgy. Like she was seeing a future she would never have.

'She's doing an interview,' Piper said. 'She told me she would have her phone switched off for a couple of hours. Can I help?'

Wakefield Senior tapped his fingers on the doorframe, as though considering whether there would be any point delivering information to Wendy's junior. 'I want to talk to her about next month's feature article.'

'This one?' Piper fished the article from her stack. Commissioned six months earlier, it was a feature on Robert Pattinson.

'Yes, that one,' Patrick agreed. 'It's not in line with our new direction. We need something controversial. Something current.'

Instinctively, Piper agreed. There was nothing edgy about the article. No scoop, just pretty much an ad for his new movie.

'Any suggestions?' Patrick asked, to Piper's surprise.

Piper's mind raced to Kara Kingston, the seed of an idea taking root instantly. There had been some pretty raw stuff on her Twitter feed after she came out. Piper had been too busy to study it properly. But maybe she could make time . . .

'Yes, actually,' Piper said. 'I just need to clear it with my source though. Can I get back to you after I speak to –' She stopped herself just before she mentioned Kara's name – 'A couple of people,' she finished. Of course she'd have to get clearance from Kara. And she'd have to run the idea by Wendy, but Wendy had already told her she should try to write something herself. Wendy was a facilitator, not a blocker like Vivian. Just thinking about the possibilities felt thrilling.

It was as though Patrick Wakefield felt the charge. He was

looking at her differently, like she might add up to something more than Wendy's junior. 'All right. I heard you wrote an article good enough for someone to steal. So, I'd be happy to hear your ideas, after you've spoken to your *source*.'

He turned to leave. Piper couldn't resist asking. It wasn't like Patrick would know that anything had happened between her and Mason.

'So, where is Mason these days?' She made sure her voice was casual, though her heart thumped loudly.

'He landed himself a position as the director of business development at Oracle,' Patrick said proudly, then added, 'Oh, and you've got twenty-four hours to get back to me about that feature article.'

As soon as he was gone, Piper googled 'Oracle' and the search came back with a company based in Redwood, California. Her heart fell to the bottom of her stomach as the realisation hit her — Mason had gone back to the States.

⁓

'So, we've really got the place to ourselves just because you let someone snap you walking in the door?' Piper giggled, tucking a starched white bath sheet around her torso.

Kara smiled. 'Yup,' she said. 'They'll get their value out of it. So, now all we gals have to endure is an hour-long massage.' She pointed over her shoulder at the masseuses.

'Poor us,' Piper said.

'Really? I think it's kind of lucky,' Georgie said seriously. 'This kind of thing can be pretty expensive if you have to pay for it.'

'It's a joke, George,' Kara said, snapping a spare towel at her. Kara's long, tanned legs seemed longer and more tanned with the white bath sheet wrapped around her.

Georgie laughed at herself. With her mass of blonde hair tucked up in a makeshift bun and her face devoid of make-up, she looked young and ridiculously fresh. Piper fingered her own ponytail and looked down at her ordinary body poking out of the bath sheet. She loved these girls, but did they really have to be so freaking gorgeous?

'Of course. I knew that,' Georgie laughed.

Piper gave Georgie a wink before she lay face-down on the massage table, resting her face in the hole.

'What pressure would you like?' asked Piper's gorgeous male masseur.

'She'll have hard pressure, thanks,' Kara answered for Piper. 'The girl has knots on her knots, she works that hard.' Kara must have lain down on her own massage table, because her next words sounded slightly muffled. 'You've been lying low since the Dylan episode, Piper. What's the story?'

The masseuse's hands were magic. There was a little bit of pain, but lots of pleasure too as he worked on Piper's computer-sore neck and shoulders.

'Working,' Piper said quickly. 'Not thinking about guys for

the moment.'

'So, I guess I shouldn't say anything else about how Mason feels about you.'

Piper wriggled on the table. 'No, you shouldn't,' she replied. There was absolutely no point in revisiting all the Mason stuff. It would just set her back. Besides, it was too late. He was gone, now. All the way back to America. 'Tell me about you,' she said, changing the topic. 'Have your Twitter trolls left you alone?'

'Not really,' she heard Kara say. 'Most people have been supportive, saying *you go girl*, that sort of thing. But others . . . '

'Like what?' Piper prompted.

She heard Kara clear her throat. 'Being told to *die, lezzo bitch* was a nice way to start the day.' Piper could hear the effort Kara had to make to sound amused rather than upset.

'That's *horrible*,' Georgie piped up, her voice distorted by the pressure from the massage. 'How can anyone be so mean in just three words?'

'Yes, that one was very concise,' Kara said dryly.

'So, do you just delete them?' Piper asked.

'Can you turn over onto your back now?' said the masseuse.

Piper turned over. Kara was lying on her back too, now, having her long legs massaged. Piper turned her head to face her.

'No, I haven't deleted anything,' Kara said. 'Free speech applies to haters too.' She paused.

'Sure,' Piper said, 'but you don't need to provide another platform for homophobia, Kara. The haters already get so much attention. Like, for every hundred tweets that are supportive, maybe two are the opposite. But it's those two that get most of the hype, you know?'

'Someone needs to put some common sense into the whole situation,' Georgie said, now lying on her back too.

Piper bit down on her grin. Georgie may be a little slow on the uptake at times, but there was something so fundamentally right and good about her that it didn't matter to Piper or Kara.

Piper looked at the ceiling while her foot was being massaged.

'So, what about your sponsors?' she asked Kara. 'How have they reacted?'

'Much to Anita's surprise, I haven't lost a single sponsor,' Kara said.

'And your family?'

'Mum was really great. Dad needs more time, though. He doesn't want to talk to me just yet.'

'I'm sorry,' Piper said. 'That must be hard.'

'Yeah, it is,' Kara replied. 'But I knew it wouldn't all be plain sailing. And at least now, I'm facing up to reality . . . whatever that is. God, it's been such bullshit. I've been seeing a shrink for years, but hiding my sexuality from her, too. I was always worried she might sell the story to the tabloids. So, I guess it's no surprise she didn't help. What's finally helped is being honest. Being out of the closet and into the open. And I just don't feel like I need all the booze anymore to mask my shit. Laurie's been trying to get me sober for ages, but I just couldn't do it. Not until now. Now, I feel like . . . ' she paused and giggled. 'A kind of post, post-traumatic-stress-disorder superwoman.'

Piper smiled. She took a deep breath. *Here goes.*

'Someone should write about all this stuff you're going through. In a really hard-hitting, in-depth way,' she said. 'The good, the bad and the ugly.'

Kara shifted up on the massage table, hugging her knees. She turned to Piper and smiled. 'I thought you'd never ask,' she said.

~

'Okay Piper,' Gaynor said, 'enough is enough. It's Saturday night. All work and no play isn't good for anyone.'

Piper tapped one last sentence out on her keyboard. She'd worked so hard over the last week, spending all day on her article about Kara and every night, until sleep stopped her in her tracks. It hadn't been easy, but she'd loved every minute of it and, even if the article never saw the light of day, she felt proud of what she'd achieved.

'Voila,' she said with a flourish towards her laptop. At the top of the screen was the title of the article: 'Out Comes Kara'.

'Good for you, Piper,' Gaynor said, glancing over the text. 'I'll read it properly later. If you don't have anything on tonight, why don't you come out with me and meet my friend?'

Piper looked at her godmother. She'd been so into her work lately that she hadn't noticed how good Gaynor was looking.

In fact, now she thought of it, Gaynor had been going out quite a lot — but driving her own car. Which must have meant she was drinking less, since Gaynor would never drive over the limit. Plus, she seemed to have toned down the make-up, and the more natural look made her appear younger.

'You look great, Gaynes.' Piper leant back in her chair and smiled. 'I want to meet him.'

'Good,' Gaynor said with a grin. 'You've got fifteen minutes to get ready.'

25

'I've been to this place before,' said Piper, as Gaynor opened the little doorway to O'Dwyer's.

Strains of 'The Lady Is a Tramp' filled Piper's ears as she entered behind her godmother. Sam came around the bar with a big smile. Piper smiled at him and glanced around, wondering which of the guys sitting alone was Gaynor's date.

'Gaynor,' Sam said. Suddenly, Piper realised who Gaynor had been dating.

Piper watched as Gaynor stepped towards Sam. She held both of his hands and kissed him on both cheeks.

'Sammy, this is my goddaughter, Piper,' said Gaynor.

Sam startled, realising that Gaynor hadn't come alone. But

he still held onto one of Gaynor's hands as he turned to greet Piper. 'Well, well. I believe we've met before,' Sam said with his trademark wry grin. 'How are life's detours?'

Piper shrugged. 'Bumpy,' she said.

Sam's laugh was loud and infectious. 'You can't travel anywhere worth going without a few bumps along the way,' he said, squeezing Gaynor's hand. He led them to the bar and slipped behind it.

Gaynor and Piper sat down as he poured Gaynor a champagne. 'And for you, young lady?' he asked.

'Champagne will be –' Piper stopped mid-sentence. One of the guys at the bar had swivelled around on his chair to face her. *Mason.*

Piper's heart thumped. One glimpse and all the effort she'd put into not thinking about him was worth nothing.

'Ah,' Sam said. 'Piper, meet Mason.'

Piper stared at Mason as though she was seeing a ghost.

Others in the bar laughed and chatted. The next song came on, a husky Billie Holiday tune. Sam finished pouring Piper's drink, then walked around the bar. He took Gaynor's hand and the two of them started dancing.

Mason came and sat next to Piper without a word.

Piper tried to keep the emotion out of her voice. 'I thought . . .' She took a deep breath. 'I thought you got a job with Oracle in the States,' she choked.

'Oh, Piper,' he said softly. 'I wanted to contact you, but I thought you wanted me to leave you alone.' He looked at her carefully. 'I did get a job with Oracle. But I'm based here.'

Piper's heart was racing. 'I broke up with Dylan!' she blurted before she even allowed herself to think. 'Weeks ago. That night at The Texan.' She gulped and her eyes welled with tears.

If she had a chance, a final chance, to be with Mason, this was it. She knew there would be no other. 'Because I want to be with you.'

26

'Hey, nice flat,' said Piper, as she stepped inside Mason's front door. 'That's a great view of the . . . '

Mason grabbed her around the waist and pulled her to him.

'Oh my god,' Piper said with a nervous giggle. 'Are you going to do a shut-up kiss? It's such a cliché on —'

There was no more room for words. Not even much room for thoughts. It was all sensation as they kissed. It was all his lips and her lips and his tongue searching and every nerve in Piper's body standing to attention. When Mason pulled away, it was too soon. Piper looked up at him.

'That wasn't too bad,' she whispered, 'but on TV shows it usually goes for a bit longer.'

Mason smiled. She felt his body press into her. His heartbeat thumped steadily.

'The thing is, there are other clichés to try. Better not to just stick with the one,' he said, gently lifting her hair to one side and exposing her neck.

His lips brushed against her collarbone and climbed up to her ear as though he was exploring her slowly, paying attention to every detail.

Piper closed her eyes and leant into the feeling of his tongue against her skin. Desire flooded through her.

'Piper,' he breathed after a moment, 'I think there might be a slight chance that I like you.'

Piper smiled. 'I think there might also be just a tiny bit of a chance I like you back.'

She could see the definition of his arm muscles when he lifted her top over her head and dropped it on the floor. She stood in her navy lace bra and his eyes scanned over her.

'Oh fuck,' he said, a smile playing on his lips. 'You're so hot.'

His hands rose, up from her waist, over her belly. He cupped her breasts briefly, then undid her bra. His hands returned to her breasts, more firmly now, as he brushed over her nipples.

Piper lifted his T-shirt over his head. His chest was broader, stronger, than Piper had imagined. They were magnets now there were no clothes between them. Drawn to each other.

He kissed her and lifted her up. She wrapped her legs around him, feeling his hardness against her. Her body pulsed with pleasure, little waves lapping inside her as he carried her up the hallway. He put her down on his bed, pulling down her jeans, bringing her underwear with them. When she was completely naked, he switched on the bedside light.

'I want to see you,' he said. 'You're beautiful.'

'Really?' Piper leant up on her elbow and stroked his face.

They started exploring each other slowly. His fingers circled, teased and caressed her as though there was no urgency. This moment didn't have to be rushed, and was important and beautiful. He kissed her everywhere, until the build-up was too much. Desire overtook her.

He reached into his bedside drawer for a condom. As soon as he lay down beside her, she reached for him. She expected him to lie on top of her, but instead, he lay back and lifted her so that she was kneeling, her legs either side of him. He pressed against her, and she wanted him so badly. She lowered herself down on him and he moaned.

Eventually, a shudder built through her, leaving smaller shockwaves in its wake. *So this is what it's like*, thought Piper.

This is what it's like to love. With her head. With her heart. With her whole body.

⁓

Piper stroked Mason's chest, her hand moving up and down over his muscles as she lay beside him. Even now, after hours together, his body still held that impossible balance of the known and the unknown. She watched his chest rise and fall with his breath.

She let her hand drift lower. He let out a small groan and leant over to kiss her.

'Piper,' he said. 'What you do to me.' Piper could *see* what she did to him. It felt amazing. His smile was gorgeous. He ran his hand down her side.

Piper rose on an elbow and looked down at him. 'I'm so glad you're not my boss anymore.'

'And I'm so glad you're not with that cheating surfer boyfriend.'

'And I'm glad you don't have a fake supermodel girlfriend.'

Mason laughed. 'So there's nothing between us now.'

Piper smiled. 'There's *everything* between us,' she corrected.

27

One year later . . .

'The nominees for Best Article of the Year are . . .'

Piper held her breath. Being at the Australian Publishers Excellence Awards was even more exciting than she had anticipated. She looked up at the stage to the MC. Around the room, the attendees grew quiet and the waiters and waitresses in black tuxedos and crisp white shirts were standing still, waiting for the announcement.

Mason's hand squeezed Piper's leg through the dress Kara had given her: a strapless red dress with a hugging bodice and flounced organza skirt. She found Mason's hand and squeezed back.

'Liza Patrice, *Elle*, for "The Devil You Know",' the MC continued.

The audience clapped. Piper looked around her own table. At beautiful, wide-eyed Georgie. At Rose, in floral chiffon. At Gaynor and Sam, who struggled to look anywhere but at each other. At Patrick Wakefield, in a navy blue suit. At Wendy, her teacher and mentor — dressed simply in black — beaming with pride at her student, and Lawrence beside her. At Kara, looking perfect in the white sequinned gown with a plunging neckline she'd designed herself, who crossed the fingers of both her hands and held them out towards Piper. At Laurie, sitting proudly next to her girlfriend with a glint in her eyes that told how happy she was, even a year later, to be out in the open.

Sitting right beside her was Mason, in a sharp suit with a white shirt and charcoal tie. Piper thought he'd never looked more gorgeous.

She reminded herself to breathe. With the breath came a gratitude that was almost overwhelming. She didn't need an award. She pretty much had it all.

'Megan Roach, *InStyle*, for "They Heard It on the Grapevine".'

There was another round of applause. Piper clapped hard. She looked two tables away, where Megan Roach, the writer of that fabulous article about the four women, rose and waved her hand.

Piper had scoured this article too. 'They Heard It on the Grapevine' was a gruesome, yet fascinating, account of people who had murdered their partners after suspecting them, wrongly, of cheating. Just to be nominated in the same category as Megan Roach, a writer whose incredible talent and respect for her subjects was palpable on the page, was a thrill Piper knew she would remember forever.

Mason's hand was now on her knee. Resting lightly but, as always, with a firmness behind the touch.

'Piper Bancroft, *Aspire*, for "Out Comes Kara".'

Everyone at her table went wild. Their furious clapping made even the very serious MC break into a smile. Piper felt her face flush. Especially when Mason's lips brushed her exposed neck. Gentle and tender and so fast that probably no-one else even saw it.

'And the winner is . . . ' The MC opened the envelope. He leant into the microphone. 'Piper Bancroft, *Aspire*, for "Out Comes Kara".'

Piper felt like she was dreaming. This award would get her into any journalism course in the country. The time she'd spent in the features department had been fantastic, but it had also made her realise she wanted to learn about every aspect of journalism from the ground up. Her eyes welled with tears.

Mason turned excitedly and drew her to him, his hands on her cheeks shielded them, giving them a private moment. He kissed her, then moved a thumb down to her lips.

'Hey, um . . . ' he said with his wry grin. 'You've got some lipstick here . . . ' He wiped her front tooth with his thumb.

She laughed, grateful to him for stemming the tears so she could get up and accept her award without sobbing.

'I love you Piper Bancroft,' he whispered.

31901056315874